ALLEN COUNTY PUBLIC LIBRARY

3 1833 01562 4577   S0-BXC-987

Fiction
Harmon, Susan.
Colorado ransom

DO NOT REMOVE
CARDS FROM POCKET

ALLEN COUNTY PUBLIC LIBRARY

FORT WAYNE, INDIANA 46802

You may return this book to any agency, branch,
or bookmobile of the Allen County Public Library.

DEMCO

COLORADO RANSOM

COLORADO RANSOM

Susan Harmon

Walker and Company
New York

Allen County Public Library
Ft. Wayne, Indiana

*This book is dedicated to my parents
and grandparents*

Copyright © 1992 by Susan Harmon

All rights reserved. No part of this book may be reproduced or transmitted in any
form or by any means, electronic or mechanical, including photocopying,
recording, or by any information storage and retrieval system, without permission
in writing from the Publisher.

All the characters and events portrayed in this work are fictitious.

First published in the United States of America in 1992
by Walker Publishing Company, Inc.

Published simultaneously in Canada by Thomas Allen & Son
Canada, Limited, Markham, Ontario

Library of Congress Cataloging-in-Publication Data
Harmon, Susan.
Colorado ransom / Susan Harmon.
p.   cm.
ISBN 0-8027-4125-8
I. Title.
PS3558.A62457C65   1991
813'.54—dc20   91-22345
CIP

Contents

PART I

The Lucky Lady Mine

CHAPTER 1

THERE was but a hint of gray light left in the sky as Forrest Bates emerged from the mine shaft. He blew out his lantern and set it on a crude shelf created from a wooden plank on long spikes driven into the rock wall. He leaned a couple of picks against the rocks and stretched his arms, feeling the effects of a day's work at hard-rock mining throughout his body. At forty-one, Forrest was still lean and muscular, but he realized he couldn't swing the pick and the mallet like he could when he first hit the mines nearly twenty years ago.

He swung a saddle on Carly, picketed nearby, then he and the sorrel started down the mountain trail toward his cabin. As he neared home, he could smell the smoke coming from the fireplace; and he thought impatiently of the meal that awaited him and, more longingly, of the young woman who was there to greet him.

Olivia heard the soft thud of Carly's tripping gait and opened the door. Stepping out onto the small porch, she waved at Forrest as he headed Carly toward the barn. She looked to see if Forrest carried an ore sack. If he did, he probably had a fairly successful day in the mine. Today he carried nothing, but she was not disheartened, since the last week or so had been fruitful. She stepped back inside and stirred the stew, filling the cabin with aromas of venison, wild onions, and garlic. Her long, blond hair was tied at the nape of her neck with a blue ribbon, and she coaxed a few flying tendrils away from her ears and back into place. As she placed the chipped blue plates on the table and made final preparations for the meal, she pondered her relationship with Forrest. She wondered whether it was fair to go on

3

accepting Forrest's hospitality, his food, his lodging, while continuing to evade his proposals. She hoped, with some feelings of guilt, that Forrest would be too tired to bring up the subject of marriage again tonight.

Forrest came in. The dull look in his green eyes and the way he eased into the kitchen chair revealed his fatigue, but his appetite seemed undiminished. After a few bites of stew and cornbread, and a swig or two of strong, hot coffee, Forrest felt more like talking. "Olivia, I'm goin' to need to hire somebody to help me shore up the mine with timbers. I went through a lot of dead stuff today, but the next day or two's goin' to give me a good-sized vein." His voice picked up a tone of excitement. "Yep, think I'll take what ore I've got down to Wells Springs tomorrow and see if I can scare up some help."

After the War Between the States, Roy Shannon had moved around in the western territories hoping to get rich quickly from the gold and silver left in the mountains, but he soon found the work too demanding and the rewards scant at best. He drifted about the country, sometimes doing a little ranch work or a little mining. He'd even pulled a couple of small bank jobs.

His last job was at a ranch in the southern part of Colorado Territory. He left after having a fracas with the foreman over a woman. He had decided to head back up north toward Denver. When he got to Wells Springs he stopped off at The Golden Dog Saloon for a few drinks.

Forrest was sitting alone at a table by the window in the saloon enjoying a beer. He had watched the stranger ride into town. The horse walked slowly up the dusty road, its head hanging down to about the level of his shoulders and its feet kicking up little spirals of dust close to the ground. Forrest assumed that the horse was either aged or had been ridden hard for some reason.

From a distance, the stranger looked like just about any

cow-puncher or mining hand that Forrest had ever seen. His jeans were dusty, his shirt sweat-stained, and his hat well-worn. The cowboy dismounted in front of the saloon.

Forrest looked up and nodded as the stranger walked through the doors. His greeting was returned.

It was not quite sundown, and the bar was empty except for the two of them and the bartender, who kept polishing the wood of the counter, seemingly out of habit and boredom. Forrest kept quiet until he heard Roy Shannon talking to the bartender about whether there was any work up around the Cherry Creek and Denver mines.

Forrest occasionally had found a couple of the local boys willing to help out now and then, but he needed a full-time man. So he introduced himself to the stranger. He ended up buying a couple of beers for Shannon and hiring him on the spot.

Forrest was pleased to discover that Shannon was from Mississippi, right next door to Forrest's native state of Arkansas. Shannon talked about the South, the war, the death of his brothers in the fighting. Forrest had noticed that Shannon looked to be down on his luck; after hearing the man's war experiences, Forrest thought he understood why.

For Roy Shannon's part, he sensed that Forrest Bates was driven by visions of wealth. Forrest didn't brag about his mine, but Roy had ridden with money-hungry men in his time. The source of the money made no difference to the look in each man's eyes. Whether it was the sharp, glinty stare of a wretched southern farmer hoping to get home from the war in time to harvest a cotton crop, a cowpoke riding off to catch and break wild stallions in Wyoming, or some miner who felt he had run across the richest vein since Virginia City, Shannon could spot the fever for riches every time.

Shannon was looking for work, and he was looking for riches, too. So he decided to go for either or perhaps both through Forrest Bates. The first step was to convince Bates of his honesty and sincerity. He did this with a seemingly forthright demeanor and a friendly smile.

Over the next few weeks and eventually months, Roy Shannon cultivated Forrest's trust. Shannon made it a point never to complain about the work or the weather or much of anything. From his first day on the job, he complimented Bates on his choice of a mining site. Some of his comments were sincere, for even he could see some small veins with a subtle flecked appearance meandering along the back walls for several feet before they were absorbed into the hard surfaces of worthless rock.

From his first glimpse of Olivia, Shannon craved her and envied Forrest Bates.

But Olivia had disliked him almost immediately. Whenever Roy Shannon was around, Olivia felt an urge to cringe. She had noticed his admiring glances, and that was nothing new to her. There was something different here, the way Roy Shannon looked at her when Forrest was looking the other way, as if he were a timberwolf and she a rabbit. She searched for words to explain it to Forrest after Shannon had been bedded down in the barn the first night, but she simply could not find a way to express it. At Forrest's questioning, she simply said, "I hope he will make you a good hand, Forrest." She shook off her feelings, glad that Forrest had found the help he needed.

CHAPTER 2

FORREST Bates thought nothing was seriously amiss the next time he took ore from the shaft to be analyzed in the assayer's office down in Wells Springs and came back almost shy a finger from a flying bullet, and, of course, shy of the ore. Forrest was a realistic man and didn't seem particularly upset when he told Roy Shannon and Olivia about the couple of men who rode out of the shadows of the cottonwoods down along the bottoms near Silver Creek with hats pulled low and kerchiefs over their faces. He knew it was probably something he might have to expect as word got around that his mine was producing.

However, the second time it happened, Forrest was a little more upset. He rode back to the cabin and was sitting there on the porch with a grim look on his face when Roy Shannon rode down from the mine shaft late in the afternoon. Forrest could see him atop the tired, aging horse before Shannon approached the cabin, and he was grateful that Shannon did not ride up full of questions. He arose slowly and went inside to help Olivia with supper. He patted Olivia's shoulder with a reassuring gesture that was not a true reflection of his feelings as he heard Shannon head his mount toward the barn.

Shannon seemed sympathetic to Forrest over supper, when Forrest told him about being robbed again on his way to Wells Springs by what seemed to be the same men as before.

"Well, Forrest, you know as good as I do, it's probably some no-goods who hope they can find gold without having to dig for it. You could've lost a sight more than a few dollars' worth of gold."

Forrest could not comment. He ignored Shannon when he started talking about the two of them moving on to find a pay-hole in more promising country. "You know, Forrest, maybe you ought to give up around here. There's gold in there, we know, but it's gonna take an almighty lot of work to get it out. Around Virginia City and lots of other places there's not hardly no way a man can go wrong for long. If you don't have money for your own prospectin' when you get there, you can always work for some prosperous mine until you get enough for your own grubstake. You might think about it." He spoke in a blustery tone that Forrest had not heard from him before.

Forrest was confident he had a pay-hole, and he didn't remind Shannon that he had already been to Virginia City and a lot of other places and had gambled his grubstake on the hole in the mountain above them. He could only respond with a brief "mm-hmm" before moving closer to the fireplace to warm his feet.

Roy Shannon sat awhile longer, idly stirring his coffee while his mind stirred with thought. He had figured the best way to get a stubborn man like Forrest Bates to continue on in his same obstinate course was to suggest an alternative, and he could tell his suggestions about moving on had ruffled Bates's feathers tonight. Roy hoped Forrest would continue his pattern of work, taking his ore into Wells Springs. All it took for Shannon was a short ride on his old horse, a word to his friends, and the ore Forrest carried would be spirited away in the hands of Poncho, Juan, and Andy.

His friends were registering other claims in the area, turning in the stolen ore, pretending it was from their own claims, and thus hoping to set up a high value for their places when word got out about their success. Word carried fast in this country; after they took a little more ore from Bates they would have men clamoring for possession of their claim sites. Meanwhile, Shannon was able to ease enough gold away from The Lucky Lady on the side to allow the men to avoid the plagues of starvation or honest work. After their worthless claims were sold for big money, they would be able to move in on the Bates mine.

It had taken Shannon more than a little while to convince the men that this was the best course to take. All too often, he had to put a quietus to talk about going ahead and killing Bates right now. He found that men of their background tended to be a little short on patience.

Olivia had listened to the brief exchange between the two men at the supper table with a growing sense of uneasiness. She had felt disturbed since Forrest had ridden in early in the afternoon to relate to her the events of the morning. A second robbery, so soon after the first, in the same general area by men who at least appeared to be the same ones as before left her unsettled. As she washed and dried the dishes, she began to begrudge every minute that Shannon spent at the table. She needed time to talk to Forrest before he dropped off to sleep. When Shannon finally mumbled a good night and headed for his bunk in the barn, Olivia shook her head with relief, folded the dish towel, and turned to Forrest, hoping he was not dozing already.

He was wide awake. She sat down on the hearth in front of him. "Forrest, we've got to talk about this."

"What's there to talk about, my sweet?" He tried to give his voice a sound of nonchalance that he did not feel. "A robbery now and then are things a man has to expect when he's got something worth stealing. It'll probably never happen again."

"But, Forrest, twice in a row. Don't tell me those men lie in wait for you down by the creek every day of the week. You had never been robbed—" she paused and then forced herself to say it, "before you hired Roy Shannon." Now that she had brought forth her doubts, she spoke more freely, but her voice remained low and soft. "Forrest, I think the man is a snake. I feel like there's vermin around when he is in the house!"

Forrest suddenly straightened in the chair. "Olivia, has he done anything to you?" Forrest's voice, though a whisper, sounded tense.

"No, no, he hasn't, Forrest." She reached over to pat his knee. "I don't know what it is about him, but he gives me a strange feeling, and I'm always edgy when he sets foot in the house. Maybe it's unreasonable, but I am wondering if he could be behind these robberies. Why don't you just pay him his wages and let him go?"

"Let him go? Who would I find to help in the mine? We're coming up to a good-sized vein if I know anything about mining. I need the man!" He rubbed his hand through his dark-brown hair, which was showing only a few sprinkles of gray here and there.

"I could help you in the mine, Forrest. I wouldn't be as quick, but I could be of some help." She looked at him imploringly.

"You, Olivia? I wouldn't let you work in the mine. That's insane!"

She turned her eyes from his. "I've done worse things to get by."

Forrest came over and tried to take her in his arms. She turned away and stalked toward the end of the cabin that served as her bedroom. She pulled the curtain shut, angry that he took her concerns so lightly.

Forrest continued to sit before the fire until it was nothing but coals before he spread his bedroll in front of the hearth and tried to sleep.

The next morning Olivia's feelings were somewhat satisfied when Forrest told her he would see if the Bishop brothers would be willing to ride shotgun for him on his next run.

Forrest rode down to the Bishop ranch near Wells Springs. He had hunted several times with Bob and Dave Bishop. Though the men were young, eighteen and twenty years old, they were the best-shooting men that Forrest had known. It seemed the two had been born with a six-gun in one hand

and a rifle in the other. It was a good thing, too, because they had had many a set-to with rustlers who were after the prize beef stock that their father had built up on their small ranch. The old man had been shot by rustlers a few years ago; and now it was only Bob, Dave, and their mother, Katherine, plus a couple of hands to run the place. But they did run it well.

The two young men were excited when Forrest asked their help in running his ore into Denver. Life was usually slow on the ranch, and the young men were eager for the income— and the diversion.

As The Lucky Lady slowly relinquished her riches during the following days, Forrest debated with himself over telling Shannon about his change of plans or keeping it to himself. Finally, Forrest could see no way to hide his plans from Roy Shannon.

His most difficult problem was in convincing Olivia to ride down to the Bishop ranch to stay with Katherine while he was gone. Her insistence on going along with him and the boys finally gave way the night before the trip was to begin. Forrest was vastly relieved. He knew that although Katherine Bishop was not expecting her, she would be delighted to have company while the boys were gone.

The next morning before daybreak, Forrest, Bob, and Dave had two mules heavily burdened and the horses saddled before Olivia came out with her small valise to be tied to Ribbon's saddle. She also carried a small flour sack, which she explained was a venison steak and a few other gifts for Katherine Bishop.

Forrest extended his hand to Shannon. "Roy, look out for things and don't take that tunnel any further 'til I get back to help with the timbers."

The four rode out of the small yard, down a path toward the road where Forrest and the boys would turn north toward Denver; Olivia would follow the road toward the south where the Bishop ranch lay scarcely five miles below.

After good-byes were said, Olivia watched the three men

ride away leading the two lumbering mules. She waved as Forrest turned to look back at her where the road curved shortly to the left. Then she clucked to Ribbon and urged the sleek little mare in the opposite direction down the road.

Within a quarter of a mile, Olivia came to a small trail that could be but dimly seen leading off through a thin patch of scrub oak. She headed Ribbon onto the path. She knew she was risking Forrest's anger when he returned, but she refused to face the possible scorn Mrs. Bishop might exhibit toward her, an unmarried woman living in the house with a man who was not her husband. Olivia had suffered that type of treatment before.

She rode to the little line shack she had found previously on her long rides through the hills. The place did not appear to have been used for years. The provisions she had stuck in the flour sack would be enough to see her through the days until Forrest returned, but if she needed to hunt for meat, her rifle was fully loaded and extra cartridges were tucked into the valise. She also had a pistol tucked into the waistband of her riding breeches.

Somehow from the first, Forrest felt a strange unease in the pit of his stomach. He couldn't seem to leave his rifle in the scabbard. Before they had got two miles away from his cabin, he had his piece in the crook of his right arm. He did not begin to relax until they moved out onto the ridge that gave them a view of the valley that led down to Wells Springs. The lack of movement, save that of a few birds and a deer grazing in a far meadow, encouraged him.

The first day, the three made good miles, although much of it was over rough terrain and steep inclines. Late in the afternoon, they came upon a favorable place to camp. It was on an elevated side of a mountain where they could have a good view over the country they had just crossed. In the late-afternoon shadows, Forrest picked his spot behind a little stand of scrub brush and watched their back trail for a half hour or so. Forrest saw nothing other than the mountain wildlife that now and then slipped out of the trees to sip from the watersheds and streams.

As the day shut down and darkness began to gather, Forrest made his way the quarter of a mile back to camp. Bob and Dave had a low fire going that was not noticeable from a distance. The smell of the coffee would carry through the trees, but it would take a mighty big scare for a man to make camp without a small fire and a full coffepot.

Forrest fell asleep that night thinking he needed to buy more mules so they would not have to make this trip so often. If he had a good string of the animals, it could cut down considerably on the number of trips that would have to be made; unfortunately, it also would make them a more desirable target of thieves.

If Forrest had been wary on the first day out, the second day brought anticipation that made his hair seem to stand on end. It wasn't fear exactly that he felt, but a dread of what seemed to him to be an inevitable attack. It came just as they were starting down a steep incline. Before them was a bed of loose shale leading to the bottom of the draw. On the other side of the draw, Forrest could see a steep climb upward as deep in shale as the climb downward was. Halfway down the slope, he heard rocks tumbling along the mountainside above them, and then small rocks began to plunk around the horses. High-spirited though they were, the horses held steady on the shale shifting beneath their hooves. Suddenly, the horses and the men heard it at the same time, huge boulders thundering down the steep cliff to their right. Forrest looked up to see a landslide of rock starting their way. Fortunately, Dave, who was in the lead, also saw the massive rocks headed for them.

With a "Hee-Yi!" he whipped his horse into action. The mule behind him was spooked, but the animal had no choice but to follow the strong stallion as the lead rope jerked him sharply forward. Forrest had barely to touch his spurs to

Carly's sides and yell backward to the mule he led, "C'mon, Purgatory!" He hoped the mule had sense enough not to get stubborn at this point. The animals leaped into action.

Forrest could see that Dave's stallion and the mule he led were sinking an inch or two into the soft shale. His own sorrel waded boldly into the quagmire of moving rock and stepped lightly through it, but his mule forged ahead slowly, trying to make sure of each footing before he lost hold on the last one he had. Forrest half-expected Bob and his gelding to come scooting down from behind to knock Purgatory and Carly off their feet.

Close to the bottom of the little draw, Forrest heard what he had been most dreading. A shot. He let the sorrel leap forward while he gave a mighty tug on Purgatory's rope. Through a blurry haze of flying rock, he saw the big stallion that Dave was riding plummet over the side of the trail into seeming nothingness. Forrest had not seen that either Dave or the stallion had been hit by the gunfire. He had to make a decision, and the sound of another bullet whining through the canyon made it for him. He went plunging off exactly where Dave had gone. Bob followed.

Surprisingly, they hit the bottom right side up. Dave's stallion had found firm footing and headed into a thick stand of trees, followed by Dave's mule, which was traveling as fast as Forrest had ever seen a mule travel. Forrest, his mule Purgatory, and Bob were not far behind.

The thick stand of trees had heavy undergrowth all around. There was a small clearing in the middle, large enough for the men and the animals to move around without jostling each other. The first thing Forrest did was to quieten the frightened animals. With the horses and mules quiet except for heavy breathing, Forrest stood still and listened. When the avalanche of rocks settled to the bottom of the draw, he could hear nothing except the wind rippling the tops of the cottonwoods. From somewhere not too far away came the sound of water trickling through a creekbed.

Forrest didn't know if the silence was a good sign or not. Either their attackers were nowhere close around, or they could creep with the stealth of an Indian. A sudden spray of shots careened through the trees in the narrow canyon. Forrest could tell they were fired randomly in the general direction he and the boys had taken from the trail up above. Nothing came too close to where they were, and he didn't want the sound of a horse or a mule to give knowledge of their secret place. He reached into the pack on one of the horses and pulled out a few dried apples provided by Katherine Bishop. The animals seemed to think all was right with the world when they nibbled on the tidbits.

Neither Forrest nor the Bishops moved much for close to a half hour. Bob and Dave held still in the underbrush, so still Forrest could hardly see them. Forrest hunkered in the midst of the animals to give them peace of mind and keep them quiet. He knew if the boys saw anything, a simple wave would have him into the brush beside the younger men quickly. He spent some time examining each animal's hooves and legs. There were some abrasions on the tops of the feet and the bottoms of the legs on each animal. Nothing looked serious enough to become infected or to cause much pain. Then, with a signal to the others, Forrest crept off through the underbrush, making a careful perimeter check on all sides.

When the three met again in the clearing, Forrest reported that the back portion of the canyon was clear. He had seen no one. Bob had seen a flash of riders heading north along the same trail that the three of them had been traveling.

Forrest pulled out a kerchief and mopped his brow. "Let's water the stock. I don't think there is anyone hereabouts now."

In low voices, they talked while the mules and horses drank. "Forrest, surely they've not give up on gettin' us," Bob said.

"Yeah. I just haven't figured out their thinking yet. You boys know any good place to ambush us up ahead?"

"Dozens of places. But I think they made a show of riding off, figuring we would be watching. Could be they are still up there waiting for us to start back up that little trail and get our tired horses bogged down in that shale again."

Forrest pulled a packet of biscuits out of his saddlebag, and the men stood musing over the situation while they chewed.

The small stream meandered off in a generally northerly direction. They decided to follow it for a while and look for a spot where they would be able to get back to the main trail after they felt safe to come up out of the narrow canyon. In the meantime, they would have good cover from trees on all sides and water for the animals. Beside the stream, Forrest started a small fire, picking from among the fallen wood that which would provide a good bit of smoke. With rocks ringing the little fire for containment, Forrest, Bob, and Dave mounted up and rode quietly away, looking back frequently to see if the smoke was rising and drifting. It would be visible from a much farther distance from up on the ridge trail they had been following.

They kept their horses to the middle of the little stream for perhaps a mile before they found a rocky ledge to step out upon, and here they were able to pick up a narrow game trail through the trees. They knew these tactics probably would not delay any pursuer for long. Perhaps it would give them time to find a place that could be defended easily if attack came through the night. Enough daylight was left to search for some secluded niche among the rocks.

Dave stopped his horse underneath a large pine and focused his eyes off to the right of the game trail. Following his gaze upward, Forrest soon saw what he was staring at. There was a big granite hillside, maybe sixty feet high and just to the right of a sharp stand of bony, narrow rock some fifteen feet south. Quietly, Dave and Bob dismounted and went to investigate. They were gone perhaps five minutes. Dave returned to the trail just ahead of Forrest and the stock and motioned for them to follow. The boys had found a way through the trees, not exactly a path, but enough room for the animals to get through the thick branches. Leading the way up a short incline, they stopped to see what Forrest thought about the place they had found.

It was as close to a perfect defense point as a man had a right to expect, Forrest thought. There was a small opening between two huge bodies of granite standing side by side. The opening was about fifteen feet wide at the bottom. The rocks formed a large roofless chamber that ended abruptly against a sheer cliff. The rear quarter of the chamber was littered with large boulders that had toppled from the sides of the cliff over the course of centuries, but they would provide cover, if needed, from an assault from the front of the chamber.

The men chanced building a small fire late in the afternoon, when the natural smoky haze that lingers around high mountain ranges that time of day would somewhat conceal the smoke from their fire. Katherine Bishop had packed more than enough fried chicken for their first night on the trail, and there were pieces left over, and there were plenty of Olivia's biscuits. They stationed the animals at the back of their hideaway; the sound of feet slipping over rocks in the darkness would surely alert the horses.

Before dawn they were up and on their way, not returning to the trail above just yet, still traversing the bottom land along the creek. Over breakfast, Dave had made a comment that Forrest spent the morning hours wishing he could put his whole belief in. "I've a gut feelin' that these men are lazy, and I'll bet they don't come lookin' for us at all. They're just gonna strike hard and dirty. If that lick misses, they'll just wait for their next good chance."

It was midmorning when they found a good place to return to the main trail. Everything looked clear when they peaked out upon the edge of the trail. There was evidence that three horses had traveled it within the last few hours, but there was nothing to indicate that it was their attackers. The rest of the trip into Denver was peaceful, although they never stopped scanning the ridges and the forests around them and often checked the trail behind.

After settling up the business with the ore in Denver, Forrest gave each of the Bishops a fifty-dollar bill. He then visited the bank, where he deposited most of the money and opened up an account in the name of Olivia Palmer.

When Forrest returned to The Lucky Lady, he was relieved to find that Olivia was back home and waiting for him. After happy greetings, Olivia said, "Shannon's moved on, I guess."

"What do you mean?"

"He's not here anymore. I rode in to check on things, and he was gone. I could tell he hadn't been here for at least a day or two, so I got my things and came back home. He didn't even wait to draw his pay." Although she looked at him with her clear blue eyes, Forrest secretly wondered if Shannon had left of his own will or at Olivia's orders.

If Olivia was that set against the man, he was glad he was gone too. "Well, that's how these men are sometimes. Guess I'll have to find someone else." He changed the subject. "How was your stay with Katherine Bishop?"

She turned toward the fireplace to build up the fire for cooking. "It was fine, Forrest, just fine."

CHAPTER 3

ROY Shannon left the employ of Forrest Bates of his own accord, in a fit of blind rage at his own men. Forrest and the Bishops had been gone three days when Shannon heard a whistle from among the trees as he was riding down the hillside in the middle of the afternoon. Shannon had never been one to put in long hours at work when he was on the job alone. He turned toward the whistle and saw his men, Poncho, Juan, and Andy, hunkering in the shadows back in the trees.

He could tell by their demeanor as he rode closer that they were not a victorious bunch. Shannon's face flushed with anger. He listened with an outward appearance of calm as Poncho, a mix of Jicarilla Apache and Mexican, began the story of how Forrest and the Bishops had gotten away. Poncho's eyes shifted to Juan, the wiry little Mexican, and Andy, a skinny runt of a kid barely out of his teens, as they chimed in on the story from time to time. According to them, more shots had been fired than during the Battle of Bull Run, and they were lucky to escape with their lives.

"I ought to shoot the three of you right between the eyes." His teeth were clenched, and his eyes were black holes of fury.

Poncho, Juan, and Andy silently glanced from one to the other.

Shannon reached down and picked up a handful of twigs and started to snap them one by one while his mind raced. He finally stood up and threw the twigs to the ground. He knew what he had to do. "Meet me at the road in an hour." Turning quickly, he mounted his horse and bounded away.

19

He knew he was wasting his time to think these three could accomplish any mission without his presence. Since he knew the mine and Bates's method of operation by now, it was not necessary that he continue working for Forrest in order to pilfer ore from The Lucky Lady. After he had his gear packed, along with a few items from Forrest's supplies— coffee, canned goods and ammunition—he rode off.

Forrest was not unduly surprised by Shannon's departure. In his years in the mines, he had learned that rarely did men hang around to work steadily for too long; but it did puzzle him that Shannon rode off without his pay. He put Shannon out of his mind and returned to working in solitude, hoping he could get down to Wells Springs soon and find some help.

It took a week or more for him to finally realize it was not his imagination that the ore sack he stored in the barn was a little lighter each morning than it had been the night before. At first, he figured he had misjudged the amount at night because he was tired. One night he deliberately folded the neck of the sack in a certain way; in the morning it was scrunched together. Someone had been creeping around in the night helping himself to his gold. He immediately thought of Shannon.

That evening after an early supper, he got ready to head into town. "It's Saturday night, Olivia. Might be there are some new men in town. Somebody I could get to help out up here." He left Olivia with a demand that she stay inside with the door barred until he returned. He felt guilty leaving her alone, but he figured she would be safe for a little while. He knew her marksmanship very nearly equaled his, but his upbringing forced him to feel protective toward a lady. "Whoever has been stealing our gold will like as not be out drinking up his profits," he told Olivia, mostly to comfort himself. When he reached town he headed for The Golden Dog Saloon. He hoped he might also run into someone who knew the whereabouts of Roy Shannon.

His luck held that evening. The Golden Dog was crowded with thirsty miners, and he found one that he could convince to come to work at The Lucky Lady. Ike Edwards promised Forrest he would gather his things from the mine where he had been working for the last couple of months and would be at The Lucky Lady within a week.

When he got home he saw someone slipping from the barn as he rode into the yard. His shot missed but was close enough to hasten the intruder. The man mounted his horse and spurred off into the darkness. Forrest recognized the awkward gait of Roy Shannon's horse. Forrest could see that the cabin door was shut and secure, so Olivia was safe.

He rode after Shannon, confident that Carly could overtake the other animal. He pushed the big sorrel into the trees and then stopped, hoping some sound would tell him which way to go. He could see nothing save the shadows of the forest; and there was no sound of a horse crashing through brush, no sound of hooves. Forrest searched carefully for a few minutes, knowing any moment a bullet could rip out of the darkness. He worried about Olivia back at the cabin. What would Shannon try with her if he had Forrest out of the way? With a growing sense of urgency, he turned back toward home.

He found Olivia standing with a rifle in her arms in a darkened room. She had blown out the lamp after the sound of gunfire. Forrest gathered her into his arms and vowed to himself to stay close by her until Ike reported for work. His business with Roy Shannon could wait.

Forrest Bates died two days later, buried under a ton or more of earth in The Lucky Lady.

PART II

Heir to Trouble

CHAPTER 4

IN the seven years since the War Between the States had ended, Richmond Bates, now thirty-two years old, had been trying to put the memories of devastation behind and reconstruct his life. Many of his friends and relatives had died during the war, and his family farm had been burned, although his family never had slaves and never had supported the concept of slavery. He had no living kin that he knew of except an uncle who had been somewhere in Colorado Territory for the last few years trying his luck at mining.

Richmond had struggled hard trying to get the family farm productive again; and each year when he figured his losses versus his gains, he was tempted to drop the plow and look up his uncle Forrest. But his roots were in the soil of the southland. When he looked across his forty acres of cotton each summer, it bothered him little that he had no money in the bank. And each spring when his few head of cows dropped their calves, he knew he wouldn't trade this for the surest gold mine. So each year, he plowed, planted, and prayed for enough rain to make his little crop thrive so he could last another year.

The house and barn were simple structures that he had built himself with timbers from the stretch of his property that lay close to the bottoms over by the creek. His cattle herd was promising. The rich farmland of Arkansas never failed to yield him plenty of summertime grass and enough alfalfa to bring his stock through the winter. East of the cotton field were two shanties that had stood for as long as Richmond could remember, having no doubt been built by some slaveholder long before his papa had bought the land.

Here lived two families of freedmen who helped him work his farm.

A spring storm had passed through during the night, pelting the farm with rain and hail. It was still chilly in midmorning, and Richmond was mending some trace lines for spring plowing when he heard hooves flying down the muddy road. Tossing the strips of leather to one side, he walked outside the barn to see a young boy from town riding in.

Before he had even stopped his horse completely, the youngster was yelling at him, steamed up as he was with the importance of his mission. "Mr. Bates, Mr. Bates!" He pulled his black and white pony near the barn. "My pa told me to bring this out to ya!" He reached a slip of folded paper to Richmond, which Richmond recognized as being from the telegraph office.

"Get down, Jason. Let your horse rest for a spell. We'll go over to the house and get something warm for you to drink."

"Ain't you gonna read it, Mr. Bates?"

"Bad news can always wait for a few minutes, Jason. You look plumb froze from that ride, and I appreciate the hurry you were in to deliver this. Let's go on over to the house first. I can read it there."

The telegram was a brief one, but it aroused all manner of emotions in Richmond. "Your uncle Forrest murdered in Wells Springs." There was no name of sender.

Richmond was ready to leave by the next morning. He left the responsibility of the farm to the freedmen, not knowing how long he would be away. He rode through town to tell the sheriff that James and Harold were looking after his place. Some parts of the South were still wary of freedmen.

Richmond knew the trail to the Colorado Territory would be a long one; but Rowdy was a dependable animal; and Richmond did not have the money for train or stagecoach travel. He rode out with a flour sack full of bacon, flour, beans, potatoes, and coffee. He had his bedroll, sixty dollars in cash, and enough ammunition for his guns to assure him fresh meat along the way.

Three weeks later and ten dollars shorter, Richmond found himself riding through spectacular mountain country. He had been used to the hills around Arkansas, but one small mountain in Colorado Territory could account for half a dozen mountains in his home state.

He had acquired a new admiration for his horse. Richmond had always heard of mountain-bred horses, the tales about how they could brave the roughest mountain trails without stumbling even once. Well, Rowdy had not seen any more mountains than he himself had before they started the trip, but the roan had proved to be as surefooted as any mountain-bred animal.

Most of the ten dollars Richmond had spent had been for the best oats and grain for the roan whenever they reached a town, because it was still early spring and good grass was hard to come by in places. He had no doubt that when full spring flung itself upon the earth, the roan would be able to live off the land.

Rowdy's hardy dependability prompted Richmond to forgive the horse when he took it to mind to nip at Richmond's elbow, as he often did when Richmond found a stable where he could curry the horse. Richmond had never before seen a horse that didn't like the attention of currying and grooming, so he was always puzzled when Rowdy bit at him as though in a fit of anger. More than one stable keeper had remarked about the horse's ornery personality, voicing thoughts to Richmond as to why someone would put up with such an animal. To Richmond's thinking, a man's choice of horses or women was a personal matter and not a subject to be discussed.

Wells Springs was a disappointment to him. He rode up early in the morning after asking directions the day before from two miners. He had expected one of the bawdy mining camps he had heard about from as far away as Arkansas, with tinny music being played on some worn-out piano, lots of loose women waiting to part him from his last dollar, and booze flowing freely.

Sunlight was just starting to light up the little town. He saw a small saloon, quiet and peaceful now, with smoke coming out of the chimney to the rear. A couple of men who looked like miners, with their jeans tucked into calf-high boots, walked up the boardwalk and entered. Then he noticed a sign outside that advertised MEALS. Richmond figured the saloon doubled as a small café. In addition to the saloon, there were the usual buildings: a general store, an assayer's office, a stable, a jail that looked abandoned, with boards nailed over the windows and weeds growing around the small porch. There were a few houses clustered around the perimeter of the businesses.

His sight returned to the saloon, and Richmond found it easy to forget that he had eaten a couple of hours earlier. He had never liked his own cooking, and he knew he made the worst coffee in the world. It was always too weak owing to the fact that he had never had confidence that there would be money for coffee when supplies ran low. He kicked Rowdy into a gallop, heading toward the saloon, bacon, and coffee. If he was lucky, maybe there was a woman there who could make fat and flaky biscuits. If not, there was a good chance he could find out something about his uncle anyway.

He walked in, taking off his hat as either a gentleman or a country boy was apt to do in a place where there might be women around. There were two men sitting at a small table to the right as he went in. They wore their hats and both gave a small tug on the brim and a brief "Howdy" as he glanced their way. There were four tables decorated with red and white checkered cloths. A middle-aged woman with crow's-feet around her eyes, her hair pulled back in an old-fashioned schoolteacher's bun, appeared at his elbow just as soon as he sat down at a table looking out upon the street and about as far across the room as he could get from the other two men. The woman produced a coffee cup and filled it with a strong-looking brew from a blue and white speckled pot.

The woman looked at Richmond with a blank expression, apparently having seen too many cowboys and miners in her lifetime. "Breakfast is it?"

"Yes, ma'am, and thanks for the coffee."

She acted as if she didn't hear him and returned to the kitchen. She brought out a plate filled with three eggs, crisp bacon, and biscuits. Richmond accepted more coffee and finished his breakfast quietly, saving the last of the biscuits to wipe the runny egg yolk and bacon grease off his plate to plop into his mouth. He refrained from licking his fingers, although the miners had left the dining area and he was seated alone.

The lady with the bun came back to refill his cup. Clearing his throat, he spoke quietly and politely to her. "Ma'am, my name is Richmond Bates. I'm looking for news of my uncle, Forrest Bates. Does that name mean anything to you? It seems he was around here for some time doing some mining."

"Mister, I don't have nothin' to do with the men around here except cook and serve 'em their meals. I try not to learn their names, and if I do hear 'em, I try to fergit 'em. You might ask the bartender when the saloon opens. Seems he knows most of the people livin' hereabouts."

"What time does the saloon open, ma'am?"

"Well, it depends on what time somebody comes in and starts poundin' their fist on the bar for service. Earl, the bartender, lives out back, and when somebody comes in for liquor, well, I holler for Earl."

Richmond paid her and strolled out onto the street, where the sunshine was beginning to take the nip off the air. He untied Rowdy's reins and led him up the street toward the stable, where a sign read, "Full services 50¢ a day," in awkward print. The horse peacefully let himself be led inside to a stall and began to chew the grain as soon as a bucket of oats was dumped into the trough. With a warning to the stable boy against trying to curry the animal, Richmond walked outside and sat on the grass underneath a large elm, making his next plans. He felt that he would rather try to find out any local gossip about his uncle before he did any checking at the assayer's, so he stretched out under the tree to catch a nap while he waited until a decent hour to go into the saloon.

The sun beating hot on his chest awoke him after an hour or so. Richmond set off down the street toward the saloon. In the bright light of the morning sun, he could make out lettering over the front boards that towered some two to three feet over the actual roof. "The Golden Dog Saloon" could barely be read from the weathered paint.

The interior was dark as Richmond's eyes adjusted to the change from the brilliant sunlight outside. No one occupied the saloon. He chose a table in the corner and sat down where he could watch the street. Glancing through to the kitchen area, he could see the woman with the bun cleaning up the kitchen, going about with a rag and wiping things down. She soon finished her chores and sat down in a straight chair and took up her knitting. He could see her fingers flying and the unraveling bunch of brightly colored thread. Richmond idly reflected that the color did not fit the woman's staid personality. From time to time she would glance at him through the doorway.

Finally, she put her knitting down and came to the door. "Just remember, if you want something to drink, you got to pound the bar." She spoke as if it was an inviolable ritual.

"No, ma'am, thank you. I don't want anything to drink just yet. I thought I'd wait for the bartender to come so I could talk to him."

She turned back into the kitchen for a moment and then faced him again with a quiet snort. "I would think a young

man like you would be out rustling up a job instead of settin'
around in a saloon waiting for the bartender to come along
and chat with you!"

That rankled Richmond some, as if she were calling him
some kind of no-good. He looked over sharply at her. Her
face was unpleasant, and her brows were wrinkled tightly
together. Her left hand clutched the door frame and showed
big veins running through the leathery texture that con-
trasted with the smooth whiteness of her face and what neck
showed above the high collar of her dark blue dress.

"Ma'am, I can't do anything until I try to find out something about my uncle." He tried his best to speak in a civil
tone.

She answered in a chilly manner. "Well, if he lived around
here long, it's likely to be bad, whatever you hear of him."
She sharply turned her back to Richmond and went back to
her knitting.

Richmond looked out at the boardwalk where a big reddish dog lay. Occasionally the dog sat up to paw at a flea, his
coat being full enough to have preserved a few of the critters
through the cold of the winter. Richmond watched a spider
crawling along the floor beside his table. He pulled out his
pocketknife and trimmed the edge of a torn fingernail.

Suddenly, the door to the street swung open to admit a
small man with a growth of grayish beard. He was wearing
grubby-looking pants and a faded shirt. He stood still for a
moment, his eyes adjusting to the light. Before he had a
chance to cross the room, the sound of boots on the plank
flooring behind the bar attracted the attention of Richmond
and the newcomer.

A portly man walked in behind the bar still trying to fasten
his suspenders across a good-sized belly. His hair was nearly
white and thinning somewhat over his forehead. He cursed
quietly as he fumbled with the suspender clasps.

The man who had just walked in said, "Earl, I'd a thought
you'd a mastered them suspenders by now, you old fool!"

Earl had finally got his pants secured, so he squinted toward the light coming through the door. A smile broke across his face. "Joel, Joel, come in!" He grabbed a rag from under the counter to wipe a clean place for Joel.

Joel crossed the room and placed his foot on the wooden rail and leaned across the counter.

Richmond could see that the two knew each other well. The bartender didn't even have to ask what the man wanted. Richmond saw Earl place a bottle of whiskey in front of Joel.

"My, what service we have here now. You must think I'm a payin' man, Earl."

"You better be a payin' man or we'll be runnin' you outa town like I heard they done over in Pagosa."

"Nobody'll be runnin' me outa this one-horse town, Earl, 'cause they ain't no whores here worth startin' a fight over. Say, do you think I could get Miss Hackberry to cook me up a couple of eggs and some bacon? I've rode a ways since last mealtime."

Richmond listened to the banter for a few minutes, while a cross Miss Hackberry messed up her kitchen again with more bacon and eggs, grumbling in low tones. The men ignored her, but finally Earl realized that he had a customer sitting at a table just watching and listening and not drinking or spending even a quarter.

"Friend, what'll it be? Whiskey? Or maybe a beer?"

"A beer sounds mighty good." A quarter of an hour later, standing at the bar with a beer in his hand, Richmond found a lull in the conversation between the other two men. He could tell from their talk that they had been in the area a long time. "Say, either of you know anything of a Forrest Bates? He's my uncle and said to have a claim around here." He made no mention of the man's death or the telegram. Richmond had found that the less information he divulged, the more he got.

Earl said, "I knowed a Bates that had a claim up close to Silver Creek. 'Round here we always called him Beau, 'cause he had a almighty big desire for women, good-lookin' ones, that is. I hope that's not your uncle, for he was killed a while back, maybe a month or so ago."

"That would probably be my uncle. I heard he was dead, and that's why I'm here. How did he die?"

"Well, he was killed in his mine, a cave-in," Earl answered. "Some purty yellow-haired woman that he had taken up with came down ridin' in a frenzy to tell us about the cave-in. Time we got there, we knowed there was nothin' we could do."

"Is he buried around here?"

"Well, yeah, he's buried up there in the mine shaft. After the cave-in, he was already under maybe twenty-five feet of earth and rock. Nobody could see any reason to dig 'im outa there and plant him somewheres else. We just carved his name on a little cross we made outa some cedars and stuck it up on the base of the rock pile." Earl looked a little apologetic. Then his voice picked up a bit. "You'll be wantin' to see Ross Miles, our assayer. I hear tell your uncle left his mine to you. It seems he'd told Miles somethin' about a will."

Richmond did not show the surprise he felt at learning that Forrest had prepared a will. "Did he ever strike anything that you know of?"

"Well, nothin' really big, son, not that we know of. But I guess he did all right. He never come into town wantin' to spend a lot of money; but then, he was a quiet enough man. He'd never come in braggin' about a big strike. Wouldn't of been his way."

Richmond got directions to his uncle's mine. He figured that might be the best place to start. He walked toward the kitchen. "Miss Hackberry," he called.

The woman appeared in the doorway, dishrag in hand. Her demeanor looked dark. "Now, look here, don't you start calling me that! Joel is the only one I let get away with that name-calling!"

"Ma'am, I thought that was your name."

"Well, think again. My name is Lamont, Sarah Lamont. I'm from New Orleans, and I think the people in this part of the country ought to be a little more respectful of each other. Now, what can I do for you?"

"Miz Lamont, I just wondered if you had a few more of those biscuits I could take with me. I'm fond of good biscuits."

Mrs. Lamont seemed to soften with the flattery. A flicker crossed her face, and it almost appeared to be a smile.

CHAPTER 5

A LONG ride led Richmond up into the high country. Although patches of snow still remained in heavily timbered areas, the open meadows were beginning to look like spring with colorful patches of early-blooming wildflowers. Richmond rode, mindful of the beauty around him but also on the lookout for danger. Back in town no mention had been made of the possibility of murder in Forrest's death, but he could not forget the telegram sent to him by some stranger.

Richmond stopped to survey the mountains around to be sure he was on the right trail according to what Earl and Joel had told him. He had ridden through the stands of aspen and the grove of pine; now at the edge of a meadow, he could look northwest and see a big granite outcropping. He knew he was getting close.

He approached Forrest's property in a roundabout fashion, just to be on the safe side. He sat up in the trees for a while and saw nothing out of the ordinary. From there, he rode down into a small dry gulch. He could see up to the mine itself, perched on the edge of the mountain at the end of the wash. Richmond could see the small cabin farther down the slope of the hill where it was somewhat more sheltered from rough weather, but for now he was interested in what he could find within the mine itself.

Dismounting, he looked at the gaping hole that seemed to eat into the side of the mountain. From Earl, he had learned that his uncle had rediscovered possibilities in a mine shaft that had been abandoned some years before. The timbers supporting the entrance were weathered and gray, but still sturdy. Richmond walked inside a few feet, examining the textures and colors of the rock. He had no idea what he was looking for, because this was the first time he had stepped inside a mine. For all he knew, there could be a chunk of gold lying on the floor for him to trip over and he wouldn't recognize it. When the tunnel grew darker, Richmond decided to return to the world of daylight.

When he found the cabin he was surprised—he had expected a typical bachelor's home with perhaps a coffeepot on the hearth, maybe an unmade bed, dirty dishes, and a dusty floor. Instead, he found a neat and cozy room, although sparsely furnished. Just to the left of the door was the kitchen area, where his uncle had built pine shelves along the wall. The shelves held an assortment of canned goods and odds and ends of dishes, cups, and pots and pans stacked in an orderly fashion. In front of the shelves was a small rectangular table with short benches along both sides and a home-built chair at each end. There was no kitchen stove, but the fireplace was nearby and outfitted for cooking with iron grates for frying pans and hooks for suspending boiling pots. At the edge of the big stone hearth, a broom leaned against the wall, the old-fashioned kind that Richmond could remember his mother using, with straw tied in a circular fashion at the end of a handle made from a young sapling that had been scraped and oiled to smoothness.

In front of the fireplace sat another short bench and a rocking chair with a blue quilted cushion. The bed was at the end of the room behind a curtain and was covered with a patchwork quilt that once had been brightly colored. An Indian blanket was folded across the end of the bed. There was a Bible, an oval mirror framed in oak, and two burned-down candles on a small stand next to the bed.

A long cedar chest held Forrest's clothes, and there was an empty gun cabinet along the east wall. Richmond wondered if someone had taken the guns for safekeeping or if they had been stolen; Forrest had always appreciated fine shooting irons.

Sundown brought him back into Wells Springs shortly before the assayer's office closed. Richmond introduced himself to Ross Miles as the older man arose from behind a cluttered desk. The man didn't seem surprised when Richmond told him he was Forrest Bates's nephew. "I could've guessed when you walked in the door. There's a strong family resemblance." Ross Miles peered over the top of his spectacles, as if evaluating the younger man. "Hold on. I'll be right back." He shuffled off into a back room and returned with an envelope in his hand. "I've got something here for you." He held the envelope out to Richmond. "This was shoved under my door one night shortly after your uncle died. I guess it should be yours."

Richmond looked down at the envelope. In awkward handwriting were the words "Will of Forrest Bates, November 25, 1870." The same handwriting appeared on a few lines on the coarse paper folded inside. "To Whom It May Concern, I, Forrest E. Bates, leave everything in my earthly possession to my nephew, Richmond Bates, who lives in the vicinity of Washington, Arkansas." Forrest's signature was scrawled below the brief message.

"I sent a letter to you at Washington."

"I didn't get a letter from you. Must've come after I left. I did get a telegram, but it didn't have a name as to who had sent it."

"A telegram? Hmph! That stumps me. There's not even a telegraph office in town. Closest one might be Denver." He moved on quickly to more important news. "I've tried to protect your uncle's property. I posted a notice here, since we don't have a sheriff or even a marshal anywhere close. The notice says that all of Forrest Bates's property would remain in his estate until proper notice has been given to his next of kin." He motioned toward a bulletin board just inside the door.

Richmond walked over and read the notice. It made him feel the finality of his uncle's death. He turned back to the desk. "How would I go about taking possession as my uncle's heir?"

"Well, I reckon you would need to send notice to the closest newspaper that would give anybody ninety days to come forward and state why you should not be the sole inheritor of Forrest's property. That same piece would tell anybody your uncle owed money to to come forward and file a claim. I could get the notices off for you if you would want me to."

"I would appreciate it if you could do that. Mr. Miles, do you mind if I leave this with you for a few days?" He pushed his uncle's will back toward Ross Miles.

"No, of course not. I'll just put it back in my safe."

Richmond went across the street to a supper of ribs and beans. He got lost in thought, and before he knew it too much time had passed. He felt a guilty stab for Rowdy, who had been tied outside all this time while Richmond had indulged himself. He grabbed his hat and went out the door, gathering Rowdy's reins and heading toward the stable leading the horse. Halfway up the street he heard a rustle at the side of a building he was passing. Cautiously, Richmond dropped down and pretended to check a shoe on the horse. His actions were quick—and lucky, for a bullet whizzed over his head and past the ears of his horse. He whirled and put a couple of rounds into the darkness beside the building where he thought the shot had been fired.

Richmond crouched low and ran toward the building. Squeezing his body as closely as possible to the clapboards of the hardware store, he crept toward the small alley behind the building while several men poured out the front doors of The Golden Dog, guns in hand. The sound of hooves pounding away from the far end of the dark passageway was almost drowned out by the voices of the men from the saloon, who were hoping to see a gunfight or at least the aftermath of one.

All Richmond could see when he peered into the darkness between the buildings was a quick flurry of movement in the dim moonlight beyond. He quickly turned and ran toward Rowdy, mounted, and started off in the direction he thought the man on horseback had taken.

CHAPTER 6

A FEW miles outside town, Richmond lay sprawled unconscious on the ground. Slowly, he awoke and reached a hand to his aching head. He could feel a gaping crease just above the right temple, oozing a good bit of blood, and he could feel a good-sized lump forming behind his left ear where he must have struck a rock as he hit the ground.

He rose to all fours, trying to get a bearing on the world. As his eyes began adjusting to the darkness, he was able to begin making out the shapes of trees around him, which seemed to vibrate with every pulsating throb that shot through his head. As his senses began to return, Richmond listened. There was nothing to hear except the noise of wind swishing softly through the tops of the trees, and he began to become aware of the chill of the night. He pulled his jacket closer around his body and felt the reassuring weight of the six-gun still on his hip.

Apparently, Richmond had fallen in a dry creekbed. Looking around him, he tried to reconstruct in his mind what had happened before he had felt the sharp crack on the side of his skull that had sent him sprawling from the back of his horse. His horse! Richmond listened steadily for any sounds from the animal; he knew it was unlikely that Rowdy would have run.

Suddenly, he could just make out the form of the big horse, standing completely still with his ears at attention and staring in Richmond's direction. The horse reins trailed alongside his neck, but each time Richmond got close and reached out a hand, the horse backed off a few steps. With despair, Richmond realized this was one of the big gelding's

39

cantankerous spells, and he felt like cursing. "Stand, boy," he whispered. The reins were again just out of reach, and Richmond inched forward. He finally grasped the reins, and the horse became more tranquil.

When Richmond was in the saddle he began to see spots before his eyes. He blinked hard, wondering if he was more addled than he realized. The white spots did not go away. Snow! It was snowing! He knew two things a man riding alone in a strange and lonesome country needed the least were a bullet wound and a snowstorm. He had already had one tonight, and now he faced the other. It was too late in the season for a snowstorm, even in these mountains, but nature seemed to have other ideas as the flakes became bigger and more numerous.

Richmond had to decide whether to head back to town where there was a warm bed of straw in the livery stable or make camp somewhere nearby. If he started toward Wells Springs, he would be a perfect target if someone was lying in wait for him along the way, which made him wonder why whoever it was hadn't finished him off as he lay in the creekbed. He didn't want to give the man a third chance at him tonight, besides he wanted to be here early in the morning to check the man's tracks.

He headed the roan down the creekbed looking for a decent place to spend the rest of the night, hoping the snow would stop before it wiped out the tracks of the man who had shot him.

After a quarter hour or so of slow riding, Richmond saw a thick stand of young pines off to the right. He picketed Rowdy and spread his blanket nearby, keeping his rifle and saddle within easy reach. He ached for a fire, but would not risk the danger of smoke being seen, in case his assailant was anywhere close.

When dawn came creeping slowly over the eastern mountains, Richmond was up, glad to see that the early-spring storm had fizzled out quickly through the night, leaving only a dusting of white here and there. He could not resist making a small fire for coffee and a little hot water for his head wound. Scouting around shortly after dawn, he ran across a skinny snakeroot plant near some gnarled roots of an elm. He pulverized the roots of the plant with a rock, the way he had seen his grandmother do when he was a kid. He made a thick paste with warm water and spread the concoction across the injury to his head. He had no idea if the treatment would help a gunshot wound, but his grandmother had used it for various mishaps among the neighbors, so he figured it would do no harm and just might draw out the soreness.

Richmond swung up on Rowdy, who seemed to be in more cooperative spirits now that morning had come and the snow had stopped.

He returned to the creekbed where he had been wounded and spent the better part of an hour trying to put some kind of story together from the things he found. He could see the prints of two horses that were not his. One seemed to be a big horse carrying a heavy rider. The prints of the other were smaller and not so deeply embedded in the soft sand. He found an empty shell about fifty yards away from where he had fallen. Near the spent shell were boot prints. There were not many, but a man had lighted from his horse long enough to squat down behind a fallen, half-rotted timber and take a shot at him. The shot had come from the trail ahead of where Richmond had fallen.

Making ever-wider circles, Richmond found a spot where the smaller of the two horses had stood for many minutes, long enough to make a pattern of hoofprints as it shifted. There were no human footprints, so the rider of this horse had never dismounted. Of course, this rider might have nothing to do with his predicament. Those prints could have been made earlier or later. Then, he saw the other shell. It lay underneath a small bush. He picked it up and put it into his pocket. He went back to where he had found the first one. Most likely, the shot from here had caused his head wound.

Crouching low, he looked at every grain of sand, every leaf, every piece of bark. He found a few large drops of blood that had escaped his previous search. They were on the bottom sides of leaves that had been turned over when the gunman's horse got hell-bent away from the place.

Richmond was perplexed. Someone had taken two shots at him through the evening. Then someone else had taken a shot at the first man and had probably saved Richmond's life. It just made no sense. Had the second gunman followed whoever had trailed Richmond from town?

Who in Colorado Territory would want to kill him? Even more bizarre, who would want to save his life? For a few minutes, Richmond felt as he had during the war, that for some ungodly reason some men had been born with an insane desire to kill and nearly any event would serve as a good excuse.

The prints of the horses led off in different directions; the smaller one down the trail back toward town, the other up into the hills. It looked as if the stranger had ridden up the creekbed with his horse running at what would have been probably the top speed allowed by the sand of the empty stream. He had left the creekbed on a stretch of rock. As much as Richmond hated giving up a fresh trail, he knew it would not be wise to set off into mountain country new to him without provisions. He turned Rowdy back toward Wells Springs. He decided to move to Forrest's cabin for now. If the attack upon him had been more than a crude attempt by a random thief, he would probably find out as quickly by staying at the cabin as he would by tracking an unknown person in strange and wild country. It would be better to let the man come to him.

Prices were high at the general store, just as Richmond expected them to be. He bought only the basic necessities:

bacon, potatoes, flour, sugar, salt, and coffee. He had seen some canned goods stored on the shelves of the cabin, and there was plenty of game around.

After Richmond had bought supplies and paid his bill at the stable, he made two more stops before he left town, one at the assayer's office and one at The Golden Dog. He figured it was time to tell Ross Miles about the grim message that the telegram had contained and the attack last night.

Ross Miles stroked his chin thoughtfully. He said he had heard of the shots fired at Richmond in town.

Richmond asked Miles what he knew about his uncle's death.

"The lady did have suspicions that Forrest was murdered, dynamited in his own mine. But she was pretty excited, and I knew that Forrest would set off small blasts from time to time. We all just figured that he had somehow let it get away from him and blew the mine up on himself."

Miles pondered the serious possibility that Forrest had been murdered, in light of the attempts on Richmond's life the previous night. "Richmond, I don't know that I have exactly told anybody that I have your uncle's will. Everyone probably thinks I knew whether there was a will because of our friendship. If somebody is out to get that mine, maybe they think you brought the will with you. If somebody wants that will bad enough and they think you have it or that I've got it, things could turn out right nasty for both of us. Why don't I do this, I'll change that notice I've got posted and send the notice to the newspaper to read like the will is in Denver. Any claims against your uncle should rightly be filed with the clerk there anyway, since we don't have a lawman close by."

Richmond agreed.

When he stepped into The Golden Dog, Earl was alone. He was glad to see Richmond and immediately started asking questions about the attack of the previous night. Richmond answered him as shortly as he could without seeming impolite. Over a breakfast plate prepared by Mrs. Lamont, Richmond explained to Earl that he was curious about the woman who had been living with his uncle.

"Well, I never seen her but a time or two. She'd ride in with Bates now and then to pick up something over at the store. She looked like a might classy woman, an' I never heard no gossip agin' her."

"Ross Miles said he thought she was from Denver. Is that what you've heard?"

"I heard that. I never did ask your uncle, figgered his woman was his own business. Funny thing, though; that day Beau died, she got the idea that he'd been murdered. Well, they wasn't anything strange that we could see. Miners is killed ever' day in cave-ins. I figger Beau's luck just ran out. Seems to me the woman was just stirred up by the death."

"Any idea where she might be now?"

Earl grinned, showing a nice set of store-bought teeth. "Heck, if I did know, I'd prob'ly be off after her, trying to soothe her grief. She's a fine-lookin' woman."

"Maybe I'll just go looking for her myself, Earl, if she can make you spark up like that." Richmond was finding it easy to feel comfortable with the good-natured bartender. "What did she ride when she came to town?"

"A little black mare with a pure white streak about three or four inches wide in her mane, a fine-lookin' little pony, too."

"Well, I'm just gonna have to go lookin' for this woman and pony."

"If'n you go lookin' in Denver, don't start in no whorehouse. You can tell by lookin' she ain't that kind of woman. Now, I ain't fer sure if she was married to Beau or not, but a man could tell she was a respectable woman."

"You think that's where she went?"

"I 'spect so. I reckon that's what happened to Forrest's stock, too. He had a fine sorrel and two mules. We went up there to see about her after Beau died, a day or two later, I guess. She was gone, and so was the horse and mules. It seemed peculiar to us a woman striking out like that, but maybe she hired somebody to help 'er."

CHAPTER 7

THE cabin was just as Richmond had left it, and he found no new tracks around. He unpacked the goods he had bought and started a small fire. He filled the water bucket from the nearby spring, returned to the cabin, and put a pot of coffee on the iron grates in the fireplace. He stood in the doorway drinking his coffee and gnawing on a piece of jerky, a poor substitute for the biscuits he had bought at The Golden Dog, which he was saving for supper. Outside nothing was stirring except for a covey of quail pecking around on the ground and an occasional squirrel flitting among the limbs of the pines.

With his meager supplies and bedroll stashed away, Richmond spent the rest of the day acquainting himself with the countryside. Shortly after noon, he and Rowdy began to follow an old trail farther up into the hills. The pines were overwhelming, and they gave off a pungent, spicy smell this time of day when their slim needles had been basking in the sun for a few hours. Richmond enjoyed the ride although he kept his eyes moving often through the timber, and up to the skyline.

Late in the afternoon, he came to a rocky trail leading up a steep incline where the prints of several animals could be seen in the dust between the stones. He left the exploration of that path for another day, since light would be about gone by the time he got back. He had seen many tracks through the afternoon, but they told him little. He began to wish that he had not depended upon his scouts quite so much when he was a captain in the Confederate Army, for he had learned little about distinguishing one horse from another by examining the tracks. He could judge the size of the animal and rider, but not peculiarities of the gait and stride of individual animals. The day had been much more pleasant than he expected tomorrow to be, because he planned to go back to explore the mine shaft.

Richmond lingered over breakfast the next morning dreading the darkness and stillness of the mine. On the way up to the shaft, the sunlight had never seemed so precious. Richmond tethered his horse lightly, thinking gloomily that if he never came out of the tunnel, at least Rowdy could break away before he starved. There was a lantern just inside the shaft and a can of kerosene nearby. He stuck several matches into his pocket. Richmond knew little about mines, but enough to know that if the lantern started flickering it signaled bad air and he should hightail it to daylight.

The rocks lining the shaft were dismal and gray. Sharp zigzags along the wall had been made by pick, but there were a few deep pits that indicated Forrest had used blasting powder from time to time to loosen the tunnel. Richmond approached the narrow end. His lantern flickered, but caught again. Dark shadows loomed at him from the walls. The silence was eerie. He wondered how Forrest could have lived in this atmosphere day after day.

Soon he came to a small cross pounded into the edge of a large mound of dirt and rock. He raised the lantern as far as he could and looked around. It seemed that yards and yards of dirt and rock had tumbled down from the ceiling above where he was standing and near the spot where his uncle must have stood before he died. A shiver ran up his spine, and Richmond knew he had to get Uncle Forrest out of the mine and bury him in a decent spot, maybe under the two oaks below the spring on Forrest's property.

The last time he had seen Forrest must have been about ten years ago, he thought. It had been just after the war had started, at the time Richmond's father had died of pneumonia. Forrest had wanted Richmond to go out west with him at that point. But Richmond felt it his duty to join the Confederate Army. He wondered now if it was duty that beckoned or a foolish young man's desire for glory.

Richmond's mother had died during the war, not from wartime violence, but from illness, old age, and loneliness. Now sorrow from the loss of his family engulfed Richmond. He was determined to see that Uncle Forrest had a decent burial. The lantern flickered once or twice, so Richmond turned toward the mouth of the cavern. There was no more he could do by himself today in the mine.

When he approached the mouth of the tunnel he stood a few minutes to give his eyes time to adjust to the light. When he was outside he looked out over the valley. He could see Rowdy nearby still snipping grass as far as his tether would allow. Off to Rowdy's left side there was a shadow Richmond had noticed when he went into the mine. He could see now that the shadow was not a shadow, but a mule, standing with head down as if asleep.

Richmond wondered if the mule was one of Forrest's missing animals, since the critter seemed at home standing in the shade near the mine shaft. He walked over and patted the animal, which turned his head slowly to look at Richmond and then resumed his sleeping stance. Richmond swung the saddle onto Rowdy, mounted, and rode off, watching to see if the mule followed. It did, and Richmond put both animals in the corral and forked some hay to each, far enough apart that he could be fairly sure that Rowdy would not get jealous and try to take a piece out of the mule's hide, or vice versa.

When he went into the cabin he noticed something wrong. He looked twice at the night table beside the bed. The mirror was missing; the oval mirror was no longer where it had been beside the Bible and the two candles. He dropped the pillow on the bed and looked around the room as if the mirror could have transported itself to some other spot. Nothing else seemed any different from the way he had left it that morning. Then he saw a few tiny brown grains on the kitchen table. It looked like coffee. He licked his finger and ran it through the brown sprinkles and remembered wiping the table clean after breakfast. He looked at the cotton bag where he had his coffee stored. Indeed, there was less coffee in the bag than there had been this morning when he filled his pot.

Cautiously, he went outside and looked around the clearing. He found what seemed to be small boot prints in the soil here and there. They began to fade as he followed them up into the trees where the earth mixed with pine needles. Near a small bush, hoofprints indicated that a horse had recently been tied there for some time. He examined the prints as carefully as he could, trying to memorize what they looked like.

There were still a few hours of good daylight left, so Richmond hurriedly resaddled Rowdy, who reluctantly let himself be led from his hay, and began trying to follow the prints. He was able to follow them without too much trouble until he reached the wide trail that he had seen but not followed the previous day. It was quite rocky and steep. He had to admit that he could no longer pursue a trail of prints, so he followed a hunch and kept going. There was no other practical choice.

He and Rowdy began to climb. Upon the slopes above, the timber began to look gnarled and misshapen from the elements of nature. Soon a narrow path cut off from the main trail. Richmond sensed that this might be the trail his visitor had taken. His feelings were quickly confirmed by the soil of the path itself. After a couple of miles, the ground leveled out and opened onto an alpine meadow. Richmond got down off Rowdy and looped the reins around a small sapling. He pulled his rifle from the scabbard and crept to the edge of the forest. Far across the meadow was a small shack that was almost hidden underneath the trees on the far side. Richmond felt it had probably been a line shack for a cattle crew or perhaps sheepherders, but there was not any evidence that cattle or sheep had been present for several years. In order to get a better view, Richmond started slipping around the perimeter of the meadow, keeping in the shelter of the trees. Many stories came to mind about outlaws who holed up in abandoned shacks, and he did not know if he was slipping upon a gang of thieves or perhaps the woman he had been hoping to find.

There were three animals in an old corral in the back of the shack. Forrest's missing stock. A big sorrel stood munching from a pile of oats that had been tossed into a crib. Nearby was a sturdy-looking mule and a small, sleek black mare, her coat once again becoming silky after losing most of the heavy winter hair. Richmond could breathe more easily. The woman must have taken them, and she had been his visitor. Apparently, the mule had wandered from the old corral and found his way to the mine.

Smoke was curling slowly from the short chimney over the shack's roof. He was reluctant to go in and confront the woman. Unlike his uncle, Richmond was shy around women. Since childhood, he had difficulty conversing with them, or even feeling comfortable in the company of the opposite sex. He sat and watched until the sun was near to dipping over the highest western peak. Then he returned to Rowdy and quietly rode away.

He fell asleep that night thinking of feminine favors, which he had not experienced in a long time. Richmond's amorous dreams were interrupted about daylight with fierce stomping and shrill neighing and snorting from the roan and the mule. Grabbing his rifle, he opened the door a crack and looked out. There was nothing he could see except the horse and the mule careening around in the corral. He opened the door slowly and stepped out onto the porch. Rowdy saw him come outside and stopped some of his cavorting. Richmond eased past the big pine that stood just in front of the steps and then darted quickly toward the corral. He immediately saw the problem. A three-foot-long rattler lay pulverized in

the dust of the corral. Richmond examined the animals for
fang marks; finding none, he went into the barn and found
a pitchfork, which worked well for sending the carcass of the
snake flying over the fence. He went back inside wondering
about the comments he had heard about rattlers not living
above a certain elevation. He wondered if the stories were
true, and, if so, just how high one had to be to forget about
the varmints.

Richmond was in a quandary as to what his next step
should be. He wanted to meet the woman who was staying
up in the hills. In fact, it seemed to him that she should be
in the cabin instead of him. Perhaps riding up to the shack
was the proper thing for him to do. He decided to take a
gift—he would hunt some elk. Surely the woman would
appreciate a fine steak. He grabbed his rifle and rode out to
the north. His direction took him up into the trees, where
he could get a good view of the cabin and the mine.

As he paused to overlook what was soon to be his property,
some movement in the grove of trees north of the cabin and
almost beneath him caught his attention. The woman
emerged, riding the black mare. On a rope behind her was
his uncle's big sorrel. Behind the sorrel, a mule followed
slowly. The mule had no rope or bridle but followed the
other two animals as a dog might follow its master.

He watched the little parade continue toward the cabin.
The woman was carrying saddlebags across her left shoulder,
and there were two sets on the mare. Shifting the bags on
her shoulder slightly, the woman reached down and pulled
up the wire that held the top of the corral gate in place. She
lifted the gatepost free from the other spiral of wire that
held it in place at the bottom, then she rode the mare into
the corral. Once the animals were inside, the woman dismounted, closed the gate, and led the mare toward the barn,
where she stripped the saddle off her.

Richmond tugged at his ear in dismay. What the woman
was doing bewildered him. He would not have been surprised

if she had returned Forrest's animals and then had ridden away on her horse. He was wondering if she was going to leave on foot, perhaps thinking that the mare wasn't her property. He couldn't let a woman go away on foot. He raised himself up by standing in his stirrups to get a clearer view, and adjusted his field glasses. After watching briefly, he dismounted.

He could see that his uncle had uncommonly good taste in women. She made sure there was hay out for the animals, then strode toward the cabin with a graceful gait. Carrying saddlebags and rifle, she sidestepped the droppings and reached a hand back to fluff her hair. She was dressed in a soft blue blouse and a dark-gray riding skirt, which Richmond guessed was from Denver for he had not seen many women attired in such riding finery.

In amazement, Richmond watched as she went into the cabin. Soon smoke began to pour from the chimney. "My God! I think she's moved in!" Richmond continued to watch for the next hour or so, not sure what else to do. His thoughts of the elk steaks were forgotten. The woman came outside once to fill a bucket of water at the little spring. Even from a distance Richmond admired the way she moved as she swung the empty bucket and he began to feel his anxiety over meeting her lessen.

Richmond mounted Rowdy. As he rode toward the cabin he tried to think of a proper greeting. He was not sure if he should knock on his own door or just walk right in with a friendly "Howdy" as if he had expected her to be there all along.

The woman must have been listening for him to return. As he neared the place, she opened the door and walked out. Richmond pulled hard on Rowdy's reins and headed him toward the front door in spite of Rowdy's efforts to pull toward the barn. The two people watched each other as Richmond held the horse back and rode slowly toward the little front porch. Neither said anything until Richmond had dismounted and looped Rowdy's reins around a small sapling.

The woman spoke first. She strode forward with a smile. "You must be Richmond, Forrest's nephew." She extended her hand toward Richmond.

That gesture caught him a little by surprise, for most southern ladies did not offer to shake hands with a strange man until they had been properly introduced. He recovered, and extended his hand. "Yes, ma'am, I'm Richmond."

"I'm Olivia, Richmond. I guess you got the telegram I sent."

"Yes, ma'am. I got it." Richmond tried not to cling to her hand and stare, but he wasn't sure how well he was doing.

"Richmond, I took the liberty of cooking some of the supplies you had here. I hope it was all right for me to do so. I brought in some things for stew. I thought you might like it. Forrest was always partial to stew."

He followed her inside. A spicy odor made the place seem almost like home.

The food tasted as good as it smelled; the stew was made with venison, Richmond determined as he sampled it. Olivia had generously used the potatoes he had stocked and had added some garlic and onion. Her biscuits would not have won a prize at a county fair, Richmond thought, but they were palatable.

Olivia turned out to be quite a companionable person to share a meal with, if one enjoyed dinnertime conversation. Richmond had never been one to talk much at meals, being more concerned with his primary purpose for sitting at the table; but he made an effort tonight.

She told him that his uncle had taken thousands of dollars' worth of gold out of the mine. Olivia related how Forrest had been assaulted several times on the trips to Wells Springs and had finally made the decision to start taking his payloads into Denver, which also resulted in attack. She wasn't sure whether the people who kept firing on Forrest were claim jumpers trying to scare him away or kill him, or just plain thieves who waited until a man had put in the work to get the ore out of the ground before they tried to lay a hand on it.

"Richmond, I must tell you about the day he died. I had just left here to go up to the mine to take him some lunch. I was walking, because it was the first warm day we had had for some time. I must not have been halfway up the hill when I heard the shots; there were two of them, I think, then the explosion. I started to run, but when I got there all I could see was dust pouring out of the mouth of the mine. Before I got there, I thought I heard horses leaving, but I couldn't be sure, because the whole hillside seemed to rumble and quake for a while. I ran back, saddled Carly—Forrest's horse—then rode into Wells Springs. Nobody would believe me when I said Forrest had been murdered. Sometimes now, I even begin to wonder. But I know I heard those shots."

She looked silently at the floor. "A day or so later I found Forrest's will, so I took it into town and slipped it under Ross Miles's door and then headed for Denver to send the telegram to you. I could see nothing was going to be done about his death by anyone around here. Besides, I was scared, too. That's why I've been staying up at the line shack. Until you came and I was sure it was you, I had to be suspicious of everything. I thought they might want to get me next, yet since Forrest and I weren't married, I doubt that I was much of a threat to anybody."

"You went to Denver alone?" Richmond was not sure just how far it was to Denver, but it was a substantial trip for a woman alone.

"No, I got a local boy to travel with me, but I asked him not to mention it around Wells Springs, because I figured it would be safer for me if everyone just figured I had left for good when Forrest died. I'm sure Dave never told anyone. His family thought he was out hunting for those days, probably."

Richmond toyed with his spoon and wondered if he dared ask about Olivia's relationship with his uncle. He didn't have to ask. It seemed as if she sensed what he was wondering.

"Richmond, I could never do enough to repay what Forrest did for me, in case you are wondering about trusting me." She was very candid. "You see, I had lived in Denver with a man named Von Chesterfield, in an intimate relationship, since I was sixteen years old, when my family died. Actually, they were killed by Indians."

She leaned forward with her arms folded upon the table, as if the story was difficult for her to tell. "Mr. Chesterfield had always been very good to me until a couple of years ago. Then a man named Charles Farrell struck it rich in a Cherry Creek mine, and he brought his daughter from a fancy school back east and set her up in Denver. Well, she was a beauty—and rich. Shortly after that, she and Mr. Chesterfield got involved. Eventually, he gave me two hundred dollars and told me to leave his house. In Denver, two hundred dollars doesn't last long. I lived for a few weeks at a boarding-house looking for work anywhere. I was willing to be a cook, a housemaid, anything. But nothing turned up. Before I got desperate enough to visit the madams, I met Forrest." During the course of her revelations, her voice had been calm and low, her face clear of emotion. Her eyes met Richmond's frequently with a blue-liquid honesty. She continued, "Well, to shorten the story, things worked well with Forrest and me, and I've been with him since that time."

Richmond was convinced the woman was truthful. "Ma'am, do you have any idea who would have been trying to jump Uncle Forrest or even kill him?"

"I've spent hours trying to sort that out. Forrest had some people work for him from time to time. Maybe it was one of them. I have a specific one in mind." She told him the story of Roy Shannon. "None of this started until Shannon came here," she summarized. "Shannon would seem to be open and direct, and somehow he got Forrest's confidence, but he was vermin, Richmond!" She paused. "It puzzles me why Roy Shannon, or whoever was responsible, did not move in after Forrest's death. Maybe they are just biding their time so it won't look like Forrest was murdered. Or," she paused, then rushed on, "maybe they know Forrest had a will and money in the bank and they want to get their hands on all of it. Only you can do all that. Maybe they have been waiting for you."

Richmond guarded his words, telling her only that the same thought had crossed his mind.

"Richmond, do you have any idea who fired on you the other night?"

His eyes shot toward her in surprise. "How did you know about that?"

"Who do you think fired the shot that probably saved your life?" A smile flitted across her lips, and her eyes twinkled with amusement. "I was quite pleased with myself, being in the right place and having the courage to act as I did." She stopped for a moment to savor the look of astonishment on his face.

"You? It was you that followed me? You shot at that man?" Richmond felt a little sheepish that a woman had saved his life.

A little rippling laugh kept her from answering right away, then she became more serious. "Let me explain. From all the things Forrest had told me about his nephew, I knew you would not ignore my telegram. When I thought you had had enough time to make it here from your farm, I started watching for you. I did not want to be seen, since I have feared for my own life since Forrest was killed, so I went down to Wells Springs every day or so, late in the afternoon so that I could watch from the darkness for any stranger that I thought could be you.

"That's how I happened to be at the edge of town that evening. I was not sure it was you that I was following when you flew out of town on your horse, but I figured the odds were good that it was. When the man ambushed you and took his shot, I just reacted automatically. I guess I should have taken more time, since my shot just grazed him. But at least it got him running out of there."

"Did you get a look at the man?"

"Well, not much. He was big, looked to be either Mexican or Indian, probably Mexican because he was larger than most Indians."

"How would the man have known that I was coming? You were the only one who knew about the telegram. Who else would have even known that Forrest had kin?"

"This is why I think someone who worked for Forrest is behind the attack. The men who worked for him always lived right here with him. They would talk often. Forrest was very fond of you, sort of the son he never had, I guess. No doubt anyone who spent any time at all with him would have known about you."

Richmond sat silently for a few minutes, deep in thought. "Olivia, I have to get my uncle out of that mine and get him decently buried, and it's going to be man-killing work. Do you know anybody hereabouts that I can get to help out?"

"Well, I suppose there is Ike. Ike was supposed to come to work for Forrest shortly before he died. I'm sure somebody in town could tell you where to find him. I seem to recall Forrest said he had helped out other miners with hard labor around these hills." She started to clean the kitchen and rinse the dishes.

When Richmond started to pick up his bedroll shortly after dark, Olivia stopped him. "What are you doing?"

He stopped, thinking it looked pretty obvious what he was doing. "I'm getting my bedroll together. I'll sleep in the barn."

"No such thing! I didn't come back to roust you out of your own place." She sounded as if she meant what she said.

Richmond felt himself becoming flustered. He had never spent the night in the same room with a respectable woman except for his mother. Without a word, he rolled his blankets out on the floor close to the door.

Richmond found Ike tipping a whiskey the next afternoon at The Golden Dog. When Richmond explained the nature of the job, Ike seemed reluctant but willing to accommodate. A short man with a near-bald head fringed with short graying hair, he walked out with Richmond carrying a whiskey bottle three-quarters full with him. He explained the whiskey by waving the bottle and commenting shortly, "Digging up a man that's been dead for a few weeks, I might need this to dull my senses a little."

The next day was already growing warm when they came to the mouth of the tunnel. Everything seemed peaceful around, but as planned, Olivia slipped behind some boulders with the horses and her rifle. She wore rough gray slacks that had obviously belonged to Forrest Bates. They were gathered around the waistband with a belt and the bottoms of the cuffs were several folds thick. When Richmond had seen her mounting her horse with a rifle in the scabbard, it had reminded him that his uncle's guns were still missing.

PART III

Shannon's Trap

CHAPTER 8

ROY Shannon crouched behind some low rocks on a point not more than a quarter of a mile from Forrest Bates's mine. He could see clearly that the three people on horseback were approaching the tunnel with one thing on their minds. He cursed softly when he saw the picks and shovels tied to the back of one of Bates's mules. Who would ever have thought that kinfolk would try to get the body of a mining man out of a shaft when he had already been given a decent sermon and even had a cross erected in his memory. From all that Shannon had been able to find out, nobody in Wells Springs had an inkling of suspicion that the claim Bates had worked was worth much. Bates had been a closemouthed fellow and a slow spender. He had not spread any money around Wells Springs, just letting go of enough to get his food and supplies.

He watched as the woman slid off her horse and retreated behind the boulders with her rifle. He saw where the horses were tied behind some of the bushes just a stone's throw from where the woman was perched. Shannon was alone, and he knew there wasn't much he could do by himself. It would take some time for the two men to dig into the mound where Bates's body lay; consequently, the best thing he could do was back off for a time and watch. As a sharpshooter, he easily could get get close enough to do away with the three of them. But more was at stake than just a mine shaft and two or three drifters, so he forced himself to bide his time. That evening, Shannon joined his crew of three gathered around the fire filling their bellies with fried salt pork, beans, and biscuits. He had to respect Poncho's cooking. When

61

Poncho got in the frame of mind to make either biscuits or tortillas, he demonstrated his talent to the fullest.

Shannon watched the big man polishing off his plate and beginning to pick his teeth, what there was left of them. "Poncho," he declared, "you outdid yourself this time with the biscuits. *Muy bueno!*"

Poncho's smile looked like a badly used crosscut saw. The devil himself could get on Poncho's good side by complimenting him on his cooking. Poncho's half brother, Juan, was another matter. Shannon watched Juan shoveling food into his mouth, which was far too wide for his face, and reflected again that he would likely end up having to kill Juan, for the man was as vicious as a treed panther. But for the moment, Shannon was glad that Juan was on his side. The other man of the group, Andy Slade, was a cowboy-type kid who had a burr under his saddle for some reason, and it had made him turn mean.

Life had been hard for all of them, though mostly through faults of their own. Shannon was hoping their lives, especially his, were going to take a turn for the better soon. He looked around at his ragtag collection of self-serving souls and hoped they had it in them to hold together and do what they were told when the time came. One was smoking a pipe and sipping coffee, the other two were sipping tequila, when Roy Shannon scraped off his plate and stood before the fire to address them.

"Men, I've been hopin' that nephew of Bates's would get his uncle's money and try to leave the territory. It would've been easier to get him out on the road somewhere. But it seems to me that him and that woman are settin' up housekeepin' over at Bates's cabin. The only way we're gonna get that money is to take him here and try to get that will. Today, he went up to the mine tryin' to shovel his uncle's body out. I want to be sure we get him before he reaches the body. I want him soon, but we need that will and that money in Denver."

Before Shannon could go further, Poncho stood up with a sneer and flicked a cigarette butt toward the fire. "Why don't we just kill 'im now? It'd be quick and easy." He had never mentioned to any of them his failed attempt to bushwhack Richmond on his own the first day Richmond rode into Wells Springs. "There's enough gold in that mine to keep us happy for years. What're we waitin' for?"

Shannon's face was dark red. He spoke with clenched teeth. "If I've told you once, I've told you a hundred times, you goddamn fool, we want more out of this than a damn back-breakin' job of digging the gold out of that hole in the hill! Bates worked this place for a long time, and most of the money he earned is in that bank in Denver.

"We want this mine free and clear so we can work it awhile, spread the word about how it produces, and show the world that we've got money to spend; then we sell it for a fortune. Meanwhile, we've got the money from that Denver bank. But don't forget, you trigger-happy bastards, to do that, we need young Bates alive for now."

Olivia's eyes grew bleary from the sun after a few hours; but she sat steadfastly, knowing if much was stirring, the horses would kick up a fuss.

Late in the afternoon the men came out of the tunnel. They were darkened by dirt from the cavern. Without words, the two men saddled and mounted their horses, and the woman did the same. Nothing was said as they made their way down the hillside toward the cabin. Olivia knew without asking that they must have made little progress in the digging. Even suppertime drew little conversation. Olivia could see the men favoring sore muscles and sympathized with them.

The first light of morning brought quick activity within the Bates cabin. A hurried breakfast, packing things into saddlebags for a noontime meal, feeding the stock, and then hurrying back up the hillside, each dreading the day's activities, or in Olivia's case, the lack of it.

Following the same pattern as the previous day, the horses were unsaddled and tied in a small grove of trees with a few sprigs of grass to keep them satisfied through the day; and Olivia seated herself nearby with the rifle on her knees. As before she was dressed in khakis borrowed from Forrest's clothing supply and wore a man's hat to protect her face from the sun. Placing her canteen within the shade of a rock, she sat up straight and peered out over the countryside, knowing if she leaned back, the peaceful warmth of early day would lull her into a sleep.

Roy Shannon did not miss a move the Bates party of three made that morning. As he watched them, he thought about his plans for spending the Bates money when he got his hands on it. He didn't figure it would be too hard to capture young Bates and the woman—after all, he was just an Arkansas farmer. Shannon also pondered the many techniques they could use on Bates and the woman to get them to withdraw the money Forrest had stuck away in the Bank of Denver.

Shannon had been looking for this opportunity all his life. Nothing stood between him and his goal except an Arkansas sodbuster, a woman, and now a hired hand. He was exhilarated.

The second day in the mine was a long and discouraging one for Richmond and Ike. When they emerged from the cavernous grave late in the afternoon, Richmond wondered if the people from Wells Springs had been right about leaving the body buried where it lay.

Olivia gathered the horses for them. After the horses were saddled, Richmond and Ike mounted wearily. They headed down the trail. Most of the way down the hillside was a wide dirt path, maybe ten feet across, where the earth had been beaten hard by the horses and mules that had traveled it. The trio sauntered down slowly with their rifles in the scabbards and six-guns on their hips. They were looking forward to salt pork, fried potatoes, and onions for supper.

Olivia was leading the way, for she was the most energetic of the three this time of day. She had just come around a short bend in the trail when she saw four horsemen, two on either side of the trail, with their guns drawn. The red bandanna around one's neck was what first caught her attention. Swiftly, her eyes swept around to the other three hemming the trail. Without thinking clearly, and with the inbred knowledge that men did not blatantly kill a woman in this territory, Olivia yelled at the little black mare she was riding, and Ribbon sprang forward like lightning.

The boldness of the woman caught the horsemen by surprise. The quick-footed mare sprinted between the horses. Olivia heard a single pistol shot behind her as she flew down the trail. She could not tell if anyone was riding after her yet or not, but she knew they soon would be; and Ribbon did not have the pace to outdistance the powerful horses the four were riding. All this flew through Olivia's mind quickly, and she reined Ribbon and rode into a wooded area. After a few yards, she dismounted and grabbed her rifle. She slapped Ribbon on the rump, knowing that the horse would head straight for home and perhaps give Olivia some time before anyone pursuing her realized they were following a riderless horse.

She tried to plan a strategy as she slipped among the trees with darkness beginning to crowd in. It was not only her safety she sought, but Richmond's and Ike's. An idea came to her. It was going to be a dreadful act, but she had to create a diversion to try to bring about a little more time for Richmond and Ike if they were still alive.

Creeping down from the hillside behind the cabin, Olivia sat for a while looking to see if anything was wrong. Ribbon had found her way home and was standing outside the barnyard clipping a little grass and shifting from foot to foot. That made Olivia fairly certain that no one was about.

She made a quick run and burst through the door of the cabin. Everything seemed exactly as they had left it that morning. The fire had been banked so that little embers still glowed red here and there. She grabbed a lantern nearly full of kerosene. In one of the cupboards, she found a large chunk of salt pork, a little cornbread, a few dried apples, and a sack of coffee. The food items she placed in the saddlebags on Ribbon.

She carried the lantern over to the edge of the forest about twenty yards from the trail and doused a good stand of brush. Leaving the kerosene to soak into the wood, she ran back to the cabin and picked up a long, dry stick of oak from the woodpile near the front porch. Inside the cabin, she tore a strip off a petticoat she had hanging near the bed and wrapped it tightly around the end of the small oak log. The coals in the fireplace had soon eaten through the petticoat and had started to bite away at the log itself. It made a magnificent torch when tossed into the stand of kerosene-soaked brush.

She was counting on the fact that the bandits would not want flames to be seen down in Wells Springs, for that would bring every man around racing up the mountainside to fight fire. In case the fire got out of hand, she didn't want the stock to be trapped inside the corral; she raced over and spread the gate wide open. It was too late now, but she wished she had saddled the big sorrel this morning instead of the mare.

Mounting her horse, Olivia raced for the cover of trees just as she heard shouts from the trail behind her. The bandits and their two captives rode into the glow of the fire, which sent shadows dancing about them, seeming to multiply their numbers. The smell of smoke and the sound of horses pounding into the clearing caused the sorrel and the mules to come dashing out of the corral gate into the confusion of horses, men, smoke, and flames. Olivia spotted Richmond right away, riding with his hands tied behind him; and on another horse was Ike, sagging in his saddle as if he had been tied upon it. One big rider seemed to be guarding the two of them.

In the deepening shadows at the edge of the trees, Olivia swung her rifle up. She took just a few seconds to watch the other men, running about shouting orders and beating at the flames with jackets hastily pulled off.

Squeezing her knees tightly against Ribbon's sides in order to steady herself, Olivia sent a shot toward the man who remained on his horse holding the reins of Richmond's roan. The shot barely missed, but was a success anyway. The outlaws's horse was already nervous from the smell of smoke and the mad activity about him—the blast from the rifle sent him spinning and snorting. Richmond seized the opportunity and bent low over Rowdy's neck and kicked the horse gently in the side. Rowdy headed down the trail in Olivia's direction. Ike's horse had to follow, since the two of them were tied together. Ike slipped over toward the left side of his mount, and Olivia hoped he did not slide far enough to get caught up in the hooves of his own charging gelding.

From her saddlebag, Olivia pulled the knife she had used to slice meat for the noon meal. She raced out to meet Richmond when his horse came thundering toward her. First she cut the rope between Ike's and Richmond's horses. Then she managed to control her prancing mare long enough to slice the bounds of Richmond's wrists. The sight of the dark stain on the front of Ike's shirt alarmed her, but she grabbed the trailing rope and followed Richmond down the trail.

Olivia knew Ike could not ride long at a fast pace. Perhaps without the two of them, Richmond could get to town and return with help. There was a turnoff to the right not far ahead. It appeared out of the shadows, just a narrow ribbon of an opening, and she turned her horse onto it, pulling Ike's mount along. Soon after turning off the main trail, she found a patch of blackness underneath some low-hanging branches. Before long, hooves pounded their way past her; and she knew there was no way her mare and Ike, in his condition, could have stood up to the pursuit of the large, fast horses for long.

The sound of running horses drifted away into the night, and Olivia and Ike were alone. Her heart was pounding furiously. Her fear and sense of isolation took her back twelve years to the morning her parents' wagon had been attacked by Indians. The attack had come in the gray light of dawn while her pa had been hitching the mules to their wagon. Olivia had gone down to the creek to fill some vessels with water. Her ma was washing the breakfast dishes. Her younger brother, Seth, had taken his rifle and climbed up onto one of the low hills near the wagon to look for prairie hens. He was thirteen and felt a great pride in being able to bring in meat or fowl for the family stew pot from time to time. He had been the last of her family to die, though the first to cry a warning. Olivia had dipped a pan of water from the stream and was pouring it into a large bucket when she heard his cry, "Indians, Pa! Indians are coming!"

Looking up quickly, she had seen the horses of maybe five or six Indians catch up with him before the words were out of his mouth. They passed him by and soundlessly bore down upon the wagon where her pa was scrambling for his rifle. All this she saw, then suddenly she dived underneath the overhang in the creek bank where years of flooding had carved out a niche big enough for a skinny girl to hide herself from the ground above.

There she sat, knowing she could do nothing to help. She heard screams from her mother, rifle shots from Seth's gun, shouts from the Indians. The silence afterward was worse. The young girl bit her knuckles to keep from making any noise. After the silence had held for some time, Olivia ventured out, thinking, hoping desperately, that her family might still be alive. She knew the Indians could still be nearby, but she had to know if her family was alive. Mud was caked about her ankles. The faded pink roses on her dress were brighter in spots where she had urinated in her clothing, afraid to make any movement to decently relieve herself; mud clung to her skirt and all around the hem of her dress.

She was oblivious of the mud and the wetness as she crawled up the hill on her hands and knees, only raising her head now and then to peer over the tall grasses. Upon reaching the top of the little incline, Olivia could see nothing moving, so she crawled across toward the wagon. Since that time, her memory had blotted out the details of what she had seen. She could only remember that her mother and father had fallen near the wagon and that her brother was just a little farther out, apparently having tried to rush in to help. The wagon had not been burned, but it had been hacked with tomahawks and ransacked. What possessions that had not been stolen were strewn over the ground. The mules had been taken. Olivia had looked around in terror and didn't know anything to do except return to her hiding place to be sure the Indians didn't find her. She ran back to the creek bank in panic, not realizing if the Indians returned she had left a wide path of crushed grass as she ran down to the creek with tears filling her eyes.

Olivia felt almost the same sense of fear tonight, except now she had a horse, two guns, and a little food in her saddlebags. But she also had a wounded man. She pointed Ribbon up into the mountains toward the line shack, leading Ike's horse. Ike was conscious and could hold on to the saddle, although he was in a state of shock from the wound.

By the light of the moon, she hid the two horses in the woods just to the northeast of the shack and had Ike stretched out soon on the worn mattress with water boiling in one of the two old pots that were there. Ike did not seem to be getting feverish, which relieved Olivia. He was bleeding slowly from a hole in the lower left side of his chest, and fortunately, the bullet had gone through his body. Since he showed no signs of labored breathing, Olivia assumed the shot had missed his lung. After bathing Ike's wound with hot water, she allowed herself to doze lightly near the door with a thin blanket over her and the rifle alongside. Sometime during the night, the soft clap of hooves outside awoke her. Through a crack in the door, she could see the big sorrel, Carly, approaching. Behind him were the two mules, their heads hanging low.

Easing out the door, Olivia led the sorrel and the mules toward the trees where the other horses were. She had no extra rope, so she took the bridle off the mare and put it on Carly and tied him to a low branch. The other animals, she figured, would stay close, where there was company of their own kind and grass enough to share.

CHAPTER 9

RICHMOND slowed the roan somewhat, wondering about the safety of Olivia and Ike. He had heard no shots or shouts, and he knew Olivia would not be captured without a lot of noise to accompany the fracas. He gave Rowdy full rein again, and the big horse leaped forward, never missing a turn on the narrow trail and scarcely brushing the branches on either side. Richmond did not know what help he could count on down in Wells Springs, since there was no lawman there, but there was plenty of the kind of help he needed at the Bishop ranch. He tried to recall what Olivia had told him that might help him locate the young Bishops. Now he wished he had ridden to the ranch before to introduce himself.

He could not get his mind off Olivia; he could go no farther without knowing if she was all right. He might be of little help to her without any weapons, but he had to try. Richmond pulled the horse off the path and into the trees, thinking to wait long enough for his pursuers to pass him. Pulling his foot from the stirrup to lessen the squeak of the leather as he dismounted, Richmond landed softly in pine needles. He placed his hand on the soft flesh of the horse's nose to keep him quiet if other horses drew near. From somewhere, he heard a noise that he could not identify. Maybe it was the scraping sound of pine needles under the light touch of a boot. He froze while listening and tired to determine where the sound was coming from. He was getting ready to swing back astride the horse when a heavy rifle butt crashed into his skull and he fell to the ground.

When consciousness returned to Richmond, it brought pain. He was being dragged off his horse and dropped near

71

the porch of his cabin. His insides felt severed from the ride he had taken draped across his horse. Ribs on each side ached from having bounced on the horn and cantle of his saddle.

Richmond tried to keep his eyes closed while his mind cleared. He could smell smoke still lingering in the air from the brush fire, and he could hear voices. There seemed to be four of them, which meant perhaps no one had gone after Olivia yet. He could not keep from opening his eyes when someone grabbed his shirt and jerked him upward. The Mexican who had hold of his shirt had a leering grin, and he spat toward Richmond's face and slung him down again. The boot in the side came next, and Richmond wondered whether his ribs were cracked. Richmond rose to his knees and lunged in the direction of the boot, only to be met with a kick in the face.

Richmond was no match for the four of them. It was an effort for him to remain consious through the blows. Finally, he was aware of being dragged into the cabin and dropped in front of the door. Someone lit a lantern, and suddenly he got a face full of water. Then he got the back of a hand across his already bloody mouth. A small man jerked him up and with a strong whiskey breath spoke with clenched teeth.

"Bates, you better come up with your uncle's will—and fast! If you don't, I'm gonna tie your arms to one horse and your balls to another and set off a stick of dynamite close by!"

"There ain't a will." Richmond was surprised that his voice could still sound so strong.

"I know damn well there is a will!" Shannon turned to the big Mexican. "Convince him there is a will, Poncho!"

The man walked over to him and stood above, slowly running his thumb along a big blade of steel. "There is a will, senor. You best remember where it is before I cut your head off and toss it into the fireplace."

Remembering his conversation with Ross Miles, Richmond lied, "The will is in Denver, at the bank in Denver."

Shannon hesitated a moment as if wondering whether to believe Richmond, but he knew Poncho's knife usually made an honest man of whatever unlucky cowpoke or miner anticipated the feel of it. "Then we will go to Denver," he said maliciously. "Come mornin', Poncho and Juan here will have found that woman and your buddy. In Denver, me and you will go to that bank while Poncho here stays outside town with your girlfriend—a cozy threesome, the woman, Poncho, and his blade."

Poncho motioned toward Juan, who stood beside the door. "C'mon, Juan, we go for the pretty woman." With a leer, he waved the knife toward Richmond and then stuck it savagely in its leather sheath.

Shannon intervened before they could get out the door. "Get that girl before she can get to town for help." He looked at the two menacingly. "And this time there better be no mistakes, no excuses. I swear to God, I'll kill you both!"

Shannon and Andy pulled Richmond to his feet and half dragged him out toward the barn. The two tied his hands to the bottom of a heavy post at the corner of one of the four stalls. A crosspiece nailed six inches from the floor would keep him from even being able to get to his feet.

"See you in the morning, sodbuster." Shannon kicked sharply at the corner post where Richmond's hands were tied and then turned to kick a big pile of dung toward his face.

There was a little straw in the stall. Using his elbows, Richmond managed to scrape up a little pile of it in the corner near the post where he could pillow his bruised, aching head. One eye was already beginning to swell, and his lips were thick and caked with dried blood. Richmond contemplated some way to get loose, then fell asleep from exhaustion.

It was still dark when he awoke. He didn't think he had

been asleep long when some sound had startled him, and he jerked upward as far as his bonds would allow before he realized where he was. He recognized the scream of a panther upon a nearby ridge. Outside, he could hear the horses prancing nervously at the nearness of the cat. Peering toward the wide doors of the small barn, Richmond could see there was a guard. It was the lanky young fellow who was not much more than a kid, the one he had heard called Andy. He was sitting leaned against the side of the door, apparently asleep.

Richmond jerked his hands and detected a give to the post to which he was tied. The lower part of the post had been weakened by rot. Silently, Richmond worked it back and forth. Meanwhile, he tried to make plans. He figured when Olivia left him on his way to town, she had probably run for the line shack with Ike, assuming Ike was still alive. He wondered if he should try to reach town, but something kept pulling his thoughts back to the line shack and the girl. He knew he had to go to try to help her first.

By turning sideways, Richmond discovered, he could barely get his right foot underneath the two-by-six cross-rail nailed to the post. A few shoves and heaves, and his hands were freed from the post as it slipped ever so slightly away from the base. The rope still bound his hands, but there was enough play that he was able to loosen the knots by rubbing them along the jagged base of the post.

He slipped down the middle aisle of the barn, holding to the shadows along the stalls on the north side. He was reassured when he heard Andy snore. Richmond grabbed him from behind and choked him into unconsciousness. The possibility that he could have killed the young man entered his mind, and he felt for and found a pulse.

He removed Andy's gun belt and pulled the limp guard outside the door and propped him into a sitting position where, from the cabin, it would look as if he were sitting alert. Richmond took a few precious minutes to grab a length of rope to bind the man's hands and feet and stuff a bandanna into Andy's mouth.

All seemed dark and quiet at the cabin. After saddling Rowdy in the shadows of the barn, Richmond was careful to keep the animal between himself and the cabin as he walked the horse toward the gate. It opened without a sound, and Richmond left it standing wide, hoping the two horses there could wander out before either man stirred.

Once down the trail and somewhat out of earshot of the house, Richmond flung himself upon Rowdy and let him run. He headed toward town, hoping when they discovered that he was gone they would follow his tracks for a short distance to see which way he took and then spur their horses to try to catch him. A mile or so farther along, Richmond circled back in the direction of the line shack. He was able to keep within the shadows of trees, skirting small meadows when he came upon them. There was only a sliver of moon in the sky; but he had noticed that in high mountains, moonlight always seemed more powerful and illuminating. He knew he could not be too cautious and risk letting Poncho and Juan get to Olivia first. He had no idea if they even knew the line shack existed.

He came upon the stock in the trees. Ike's horse and Carly had been tied loosely, tightly enough for a good horse to know he was expected to stay there, yet loosely enough to break away easily if trouble came. The mare and the mules were nearby. A quick search around through the trees did not reveal anything to indicate that the two men had found the place yet.

He hesitated to approach the shack. The two men might already be inside, although he doubted it. If Olivia was inside and did not know the identity of anyone approaching, she might shoot. As he stepped out of the shadows of the trees and drew closer, he stopped every few steps so that anyone watching him would know that he was not creeping up with harmful intent.

Soon the door opened a crack, and he heard Olivia's voice. "Come in closer, mister, and don't reach for that gun."

Richmond identified himself. Olivia threw open the door, and he ran inside. Olivia was standing beside the door with her rifle, and she slammed the door behind him and dropped the latch into place.

With relief, Richmond could see that she had not been hurt, and Ike stood to one side holding Olivia's pistol. "Good God! I didn't know if I would find you alive or not!"

Ike smiled weakly and sank down onto a rickety chair. "I don't kill easy. The bullet went clear through."

They were in near darkness, the only light being a soft glow from coals in the fireplace. Even in the dimness, Olivia could see the gashes on Richmond's tanned face, the severe swelling around the lips and his left eye, and that his shirt was half off. There was a flannel shirt hanging on a nail in the shadows, which Olivia pulled down and tossed toward Richmond.

"Richmond, I recognized Roy Shannon in that bunch!" Ike spoke urgently. "Me and Olivia both recognized him, and Olivia thinks she knows who some of the others are."

"Tell me about it later. We've gotta get out of here quick. The two Mexicans lit out earlier looking for you. I guess they headed toward town first, but I don't know how soon they would have turned back. Maybe we're lucky and they're not much good as trackers. What they're up to is this: they figured on taking me back to the bank in Denver where they think Forrest's will is and where he was putting his money. They were going to hold Olivia under a knife until I checked out the money and turned it over to the bunch. Then I guess they'd see to it that I signed the claim over to them."

During the brief conversation, Richmond had spied more firearms. There were a couple of rifles leaned up against the wall next to the door. Richmond motioned to them, but before he could ask, Olivia spoke up.

"Those were Forrest's. When he died, I brought them up here and hid them."

"Ammunition?"

"Plenty."

Richmond looked sideways at Ike, but even in the semidarkness, Ike caught the glance. "I know what you're wondering, but I can ride."

"Yeah, Ike, but how fast and for how long?"

"I'll be okay," he said with finality.

"You won't have to ride too far, according to my plan. Could you make it to the Bishop ranch while Olivia and I head for Denver?"

Richmond built up the fire so that a thick stream of smoke was coming from the chimney and would still be visible by morning if it took their expected visitors that long to locate the shack. He had Olivia light a lantern. The fire and lantern lit up the room so that light was visible through the cracks around the door, making it look as somebody would expect it to if a woman and a wounded man were inside. It would buy some time for their getaway if the Mexicans had to slip up on the shack wondering if someone was watching for them with a rifle.

Olivia gathered together the small amount of food and put on an old worn jacket. Both she and Richmond rolled up one blanket each, both of them frazzled around the edges, to serve as bedrolls.

"Richmond," Olivia said quietly. "Why don't we just stay here and meet them head-on? We could hold them off."

"I'm not sure we could, Olivia, not from inside. Our backside would not be protected. It would be too easy for them to circle around from behind and make a torch of this place, with all these old dried-out timbers. This way, if we ride hard and keep a good watch, there's a good chance we would know if they were getting near us. And we need to get to that bank in Denver as soon as possible and have a sheriff or officer of the bank put a hold on Forrest's account until we can get the will from Ross Miles and get this cleared up."

He turned to look at her with greater seriousness. "Olivia, I don't doubt that they might try to go into the Denver bank pretending to be Forrest Bates's kin and clean out the account. You see, I had my identification papers from the war stashed in the back of the Bible at the cabin. If they found those, they can walk right into a bank and claim that one or the other of them is Forrest Bates's legitimate heir." He hesitated. "It was a foolish hiding place—that's the first place anybody would look for anything of family importance."

"Then you're right, Richmond. Let's go."

"Ike, you're sure you can make it?"

"I am. It won't be long before I'll have the Bishop boys settin' out on your trail, as soon as they can get to Ross Miles to get that will."

When they reached the animals among the trees, they saddled them quickly and stashed their grub in the saddlebags, and Richmond and Olivia tied the blankets securely behind their saddles.

Ike took off toward the Bishops' place on the other side of town, following an old game trail. He knew the trails probably crisscrossed all the way down the hillside so that he could keep to them most of the way to Wells Springs.

Olivia and Richmond turned their horses toward Denver. Olivia rode Carly and led Ribbon by an old frayed rope that they had found in the makeshift stable at the line shack. The mules followed. This would provide a broad trail for the trackers, who would not be able to tell how many riders there were if they were not expert. Olivia had recalled a high valley nearby where they could leave the extra animals in a place with a good supply of grass and water, and a bottleneck entrance that would discourage wandering by a calm little mare and two lazy mules.

When they came to the large boulder marking the place for ascent into the high valley, Richmond turned off, leading the mare with the mules following. Olivia kept to the trail, leaving one set of prints. They hoped this would further confuse and frustrate the riders behind them. She had told Richmond as best she could the way to find a trail that would intersect the one on which she rode.

Olivia rode along at a fast clip, glad she had Forrest's powerful, long-winded sorrel. She was depressed at leaving Ribbon behind, although she felt sure the mare wouldn't wander far and would be there for them to pick up later.

Olivia kept her ears alert for strange sounds along the way in the forest around her. She watched for any unexpected movement among the birds flitting through the trees. Never at any time in her life had she been as grateful for her background, which now might save her life. A childhood spent on a farm had given her an early familiarity with the outdoors and with animals. As a child, she had learned not only to ride horses, but to saddle and care for them. She and her brother had become very competitive as to who could ride better. When it looked as if Olivia's horsemanship would surpass her brother's because of her agility and her innate sense of being able to flow with the movement of the animals, her father introduced them to a sport at which he was sure his son would excel. He began to take the children out regularly when Olivia was about nine years old to teach them marksmanship. She and her brother were drilled diligently on the use and handling of many kinds of guns, from modern-day repeaters to the old muzzle-loader that had belonged to their grandfather.

First they shot for months at still targets, then advanced with their skills to hunting. The family's table was always laden with fresh venison, rabbit, squirrel, duck, or quail. The competition between brother and sister was so fierce, and the children such apt marksmen, that even the tables of the poorer families living close by held an abundance of fresh game. Olivia had realized that her father felt a mixture of intense pride in her abilities and yet a sense of frustration

when he could see that soon his daughter's skills with firearms would far surpass those of her brother. When she later
found herself living under the protection of Von Chesterfield
in Denver, she was allowed to indulge in the sports of riding,
shooting, and hunting. Indeed, Chesterfield had encouraged
her, for it built upon his vanity that she had quite a reputation among his cronies for adeptness at the skills western
men thought so valuable.

The early-morning shade from the trees made for a chilly
trip as Carly trotted along at a pace that seemed to make the
air breeze by Olivia. She pulled the jacket that had belonged
to Forrest close to her chest to block the wind, and let her
mind rove. Before she knew it, Richmond Bates filled her
thoughts. She mused now over the tightness of his plans and
his cool attitude in a situation that could bring death to them
both.

She tried to figure out what was different about him from
the men she had met in Denver. There was a sincerity that
she had seen in few people. He did not try to present himself
in any manner to impress others. He had a type of assurance,
a boldness in spite of his lack of familiarity with the countryside. And, she had to admit to herself, he showed a respect
toward her that she had not seen from another man. Richmond had ridden off with the stock without even cautioning
her to be careful. His confidence in her made her feel
good—about herself, about him.

Soon Olivia could see Richmond coming toward her
through the trees, deliberately making himself visible to her
from some distance. She slowed Carly to a canter and
watched him approach, sitting gracefully upon the spirited
Rowdy and looking comfortable in the saddle in spite of his
bruises and gashes. The trail was wide enough here that the
two horses could run abreast, and Rowdy swung in alongside
Carly.

"See anything?" she asked.

"Nothing so far."

CHAPTER 10

THE sky had started to fill with a pink glow shortly before Richmond joined Olivia on the trail. Richmond was grateful for the daylight, so they could make better time. He studied the countryside as they rode; he had never had time or a reason to get this far away from the mine.

They approached a stream, about a foot deep and three feet across. Richmond slowed Rowdy, and they stopped near the edge of the water. The horses stuck their noses in eagerly. Richmond dismounted to fill the one canteen that they had taken to the mine with them yesterday.

"Olivia, it's kind of early to stop for a rest, but we've not eaten anything all night. I want you to tell me all you can remember about this part of the country, in case we get caught by surprise. And tell me what you know about this man Roy Shannon and the men riding with him."

They led their horses into the trees behind a thick clump of juniper. There they lit a tiny fire, just large enough to boil coffee in the small pot Olivia had brought from the line shack. Richmond measured out a few precious grains—the brew would be weak, but warming.

While Olivia chewed on a cold piece of cornbread, she told Richmond everything she knew about Roy Shannon, which was not much more than she told him before. "But Richmond, the main one you ought to be worried about is the man called Poncho. When I saw him last night I was sure that he was the one who shot at you in Wells Springs.

"Folks say his mother was Mexican and his father Apache. Poncho took on the meanest streak of the whole Apache nation, from what I hear. He keeps that knife of his sharper than those Arkansas toothpicks I've heard about, and he uses it every chance he gets. Juan is mean, but he mostly follows along with his brother, doing whatever Poncho puts him up to. The white kid with them would probably be Andy Slade. I've never seen him that I know of, but he has a real bad reputation. Shannon must be even worse than I gave him credit for if he's leading a band like that."

"Now tell me all you can remember about the country between here and Denver."

In as few words as possible, Olivia described what she could recall about the route they were following, answering as accurately as possible Richmond's questions about the height of the passes, the location of branching canyons, good cover, and streams.

"What's our plan, Richmond, if they start to catch up to us?"

"Depends on how short they catch us. If they're close, we run like hell, for that would mean they've been pushing their horses harder than we've pushed ours, and from what I saw of their horses, they didn't have any thoroughbreds by a damn sight. Keep your eyes open and try to memorize every possible place we could return to and make a stand if they turn up on the trail in front of us.

"It's not likely, but during the war we got caught by surprise that way a few times. Sometimes we had a skirmish, sometimes we had to retreat. You and me would be better off to retreat if we can remember a place to retreat to."

He dug a hole, buried their small fire, and placed a good-sized stone upon it.

By midafternoon, they were upon a high ridge from which they could see a wide expanse of the country they had just traveled. The trail here wound behind some large boulders that looked as if they teetered precariously on the edge of the steep mountainside. Silently, Richmond and Olivia stopped behind the boulders, slipped off their horses, and peered over the edge of the rocks for a few moments. They felt slightly at ease when they saw no sign of movement. They remounted and continued riding. The trail took a moderate dip just beyond the overlook, and about thirty yards into the dip there was a small stretch of grass and a few oak trees. A spring trickled out of the rocks toward the back of the dip and formed a small pool in the shade of the trees. They both agreed it would be better to stop here for a two- or three-hour rest for the horses while the sun was still up. Both knew the skimpy blankets they carried would not keep them warm enough to sleep at night in these mountains. Here, they could see anyone coming from behind soon enough to be able to resaddle their horses and slip away. They took turns stretching out in the warm sunshine and watching the valley below them.

Olivia slept first. The sun was warm on her back as she lay stretched out on the rough blanket that she had spread in a sunny, grassy area. Sound sleep evaded her, but it was comforting to doze, feeling they were safe for some short period of time. As soon as they had stopped, she and Richmond had both eaten a bit of jerked beef. Now it felt as if it had grown in her stomach to twice its size, but at least her stomach was no longer growling. As she drifted off into a hazy fog, she wished she had learned more about food available from the plants that grew abundantly throughout the mountains.

During her watch, when it was Richmond's turn to stretch out in the sun, she kept thinking about the slab of salt pork in the saddlebag and the flour that would make a filling gravy. As the sun began to slip farther toward the western hills, she began to hear small stirrings from the wooded cove where Richmond slept. Looking over, she saw him sitting up, rubbing his shoulder and touching his swollen face delicately.

Soon they were on the trail again, looking for a secluded stand of trees where they could fry their salt pork as soon as the sun began to dip behind the hills. When they found the right spot, near another of the countless streams that run through the mountains in the springtime, they could be sure that smoke from their fire would not carry far in their location. Olivia sliced some of the pork and boiled it a few minutes in order to remove some of the salt before she plopped it into the frying pan. Richmond bathed his swollen face with warm water. In spite of the bruises and gashes, he managed a broad smile when Olivia stirred some flour and a little water into the pork drippings and presented him with a thick gravy. It was somewhat weak, since there was no milk to put into it, but it was warm and took the edge off his hunger.

Since no pursuers had been seen, both began to wonder if this flight had been necessary, but not to the extent that either was tempted to turn back.

Roy Shannon was stomping mad when he found out how they had been fooled at the line shack. The dwindling night had been very cold by the time he and still slightly addled Andy had run upon Poncho and Juan and the four of them set out after the fresh tracks up the mountainside. They had not had to track closely, for they could see the general direction their escaped prisoner had taken. It was mostly a matter of following a dim trail upward where occasionally they could see that a branch here and there had been freshly broken. Shannon had seen enough time in the Rockies to know that the few hours just before dawn were the coldest of the day, but standing in the cold watching the smoke curl from the chimney of the little shack and seeing the flickering of lantern light around the cracks of the door did nothing to improve his frame of mind. When the creeping across the clearing and bursting into the little hut gave barren results, his temper flared, and his men knew to give him time to work off his anger. They retired to the trees where their horses were and watched him pacing about kicking doorposts and rocks, glad to be out of the range of the tip of his boots.

They listened to Shannon vowing death to Richmond Bates and the blond woman riding with him.

Shannon eventually led them away from the shack, following an idea about which way they had gone rather than trying to follow prints in the dim light of a setting moon. It was Poncho who pointed out to him the tracks of several animals heading northeast and the tracks of one horse heading south back toward Wells Springs.

Two of the horsemen, Shannon and Andy Slade, rode toward the northeast with a flourish of hooves, while Poncho and Juan followed the lone set of prints going south.

The trail had looked dark to Ike since he had set upon it. The trees passed by in murky shadows. He knew the morning sun would soon be rising to set the trees ajingle with frosty dewdrops. He didn't feel he would ever be much ajingle to anything again. Turned out he was right.

The rope across the trail rose up out of nowhere, just as the gray of morning was appearing across the tops of the mountains to his left. His horse saw it as the curled spirals of rope pulled taut in front of his hooves. With a sailing leap, the horse cleared the rope, and a horseman of Ike's caliber could have made it easily if it had not been for the weakness he felt from his wound. As the horse bounded over the tightening death-thread, Ike tumbled off into the bushes. His weakness probably saved him from crushing his skull on a rock as he tumbled end over end. His limp figure hurtled through the morning grayness. He finally came to a stop against a large clump of juniper. The next sound he heard could have been a few hours or a few minutes later, for all he knew. The click of the gun between his eyes gave no indication of time. Ike's ears were alert. He heard the click of the gun being cocked and the sound of another pair of feet approaching. He kept his eyes tightly closed, hoping they were not darting around in their sockets to show that he was conscious. He heard the men talk.

"Wanna blow him away now?"

"What for? If he's breathin', he might know somethin'."

Suddenly, his head was tilted backward by strong hands behind his neck. He felt water pouring into his nostrils and could not keep from coughing and sneezing.

"There, damn you, that'll teach you to play possum with us!"

Ike stared into the big pockmarked face of Poncho grinning down at him. He tried to keep silent as Poncho began kicking him over and over again. Ike made one sudden lurch toward Poncho, which took the last ounce of strength he had. Grabbing a sturdy piece of fallen log, he rose and swung hard. There was a sudden thwack from the end of the crude weapon as Poncho's arm intercepted the log before it could crash against the side of his skull. With the sudden thrust, Ike's knees buckled. He saw Poncho's gun coming up and leveling at him. Ike's head exploded with fragments flying among the pine needles and rocks around him. Poncho gave his body a swift kick and two more shots.

Poncho walked away and started building a fire not ten feet away from Ike's body.

Juan stared at Poncho with dark and brooding eyes. "What'd you kill 'im for?"

"Huh?" Poncho looked up from the small blaze that was beginning to take hold of some of the dried branches and twigs he had collected.

"I said, why'd you kill 'im. Now we don't have any way of knowin' where he was goin' or where Bates and the girl went."

Poncho's eyes glimmered in the early-morning light as he fanned the small fire and opened his canteen to pour water for coffee into the small tin pot he had pulled from his saddlebag. "I killed him because I wanted to, he made me mad. I reckon we can figure out where Bates and the girl are headed. We want to get back out there and ride with Shan-

COLORADO RANSOM ■ 87

non. Don't want him gettin' the ones that's got control of the money less'n I'm there too."

The coffee boiled soon, and Poncho and Juan drained their cups quickly. After kicking dirt over the ashes of their small fire, they mounted up and rode northeast.

The sun was quickly breaking through the trees and spreading a rosy glow over Ike's ashen face. He had not even lived until good sunup.

Roy Shannon felt that he and his boys were imminent victors, but he could not help being impressed by the trail Richmond and Olivia had tried to set. He knew the mixed horse and mule tracks would have signaled almost anybody that a small mining crew or a couple of prospectors had come through. But Shannon could read through all the tricks, although it took him some time. He promised himself that he would get the money, the mine, and see Richmond Bates and the girl both dead. His mind was frenzied with the thought. But he had set himself a far more difficult task than he yet realized.

CHAPTER 11

MORNING of the third day found Olivia and Richmond nearing Denver. The trip had taken longer than Richmond had expected, but they had stopped often to rest their horses. The trip had been almost pleasant in spite of things, as he got to know Olivia better. Nearing town, Olivia began to grow more conscious of her appearance—a woman dressed in faded khakis that had never fit her in the beginning, her hair a tangled mess.

"Richmond, could we put off going to that bank for a while? I want to present the better side of me in town." Her voice sounded small and wheedling even to her.

Richmond looked at her with disbelief. "You what?"

"Richmond, I'm not going into town looking as I do now." She sat on her horse stubbornly.

"What do you propose to do about it, then?" Richmond knew he had twenty dollars in his jeans, which Shannon and his men had not taken from him. He didn't expect that amount would go far toward outfitting a lady for Denver life. He told her as much.

"Richmond, let me borrow the money. I can pay you back as soon as we get to town. I have a two-thousand-dollar bank account down there in town that Forrest started for me. He didn't ever want me to be in the shape I was when he met me."

This was the first time Richmond had heard of a bank account in her name. He sat silently and stared at her for a few moments.

She took his silence as agreement. "Richmond, there's a stream close to town. From there, you could slip into town and buy me a dress and a decent pair of shoes." Her eyes fixed on him with a mournful, deprived look, after she tucked her smile away somewhere.

"Olivia, this is foolish. What if Shannon and Poncho come along after I leave and find you here?" Richmond asked, but her mind was made up.

While Richmond was gone, she washed her underwear and her hair in the stream; they dried quickly in the sunlight. Two hours later, Richmond returned with a blue dress. It had a dipped waistline, and the bodice sported a small collar of lace that stood up around her neck and brushed against the braided, blond coil of hair on her neck.

She was surprised when she stepped out of the bushes where she had been dressing and saw Richmond sporting a clean, blue plaid shirt. He had dusted his hat and jeans and was rubbing his boots with saliva and a snatch of grass he had pulled from the edge of the streambed. The stubble that had been on his chin for the last few days was beginning to look like a respectable beard.

"Where did you get that shirt?" She didn't remember any shops for men on this side of town.

He grinned a crooked little smile. "I found it on a clothesline. There were several other ones there, so I figured the gent it belonged to could spare one."

She was aware of men's heads turning to stare at them as she and Richmond rode down Denver's busiest street. Carly was not the usual type of horse that a lady rode, and men glanced enviously at the big sorrel as often as they looked admiringly at Olivia.

It was late morning when Olivia and Richmond walked into the bank and asked to see the manager. They were escorted to a large desk in the far corner of the building and invited to sit until Mr. Cavenaugh could be with them.

Cavenaugh turned out not to be what either of them expected. Bankers in the West were usually portly, bald or graying, with spectacles clinging to a reddish nose. Mr. Cavenaugh was young, probably twenty-seven or twenty-eight, Richmond guessed. His hair was thick and dark blond. His figure was not at all portly, but rather on the slim side, and he wore an immaculate tweed suit. The six-gun he wore on his hip surprised both Olivia and Richmond. They spotted it underneath the jacket and glanced at each other.

"Good morning to you both!" His greeting seemed in the best of manners, but his eyes sweeping Olivia's body were not.

"Mr. Cavenaugh," Richmond began, "I'm here about an account my uncle had with your bank. I wish to take claim of it, if possible. My uncle's name was Forrest Bates. I am his nephew, Richmond Bates. My uncle died some time back."

Carlton Cavenaugh cleared his throat and reached for a cigar, offering one to Richmond at the same time. His pause was a long one and caused Olivia and Richmond to look around the room, trying to appear at ease.

"Well, we seem to have a plethora of Richmond Bateses around."

Richmond was not sure what a plethora meant, so he just looked calmly at Carlton Cavenaugh. "What do you mean, sir?" His gaze was meant to be so direct as to cause Mr. Cavenaugh discomfort. As well as Richmond could tell, it didn't seem to work.

Cavenaugh leaned forward, holding his cigar between his thumb and forefinger, tipping at ashes that were nonexistent. "Mr. Bates, another man claiming to be Richmond Bates was in here earlier this morning trying to lay claim to the Forrest Bates account. He had identification showing that he actually was Richmond Bates. I've seen no such identification from you. What can you show me?"

Richmond knew it was futile to explain that his identification had been stolen. Instead he stood up to his full height and leaned over the desk toward Carlton Cavenaugh. His fist pounded upon the desk top. His voice thundered. "If you released my uncle's money, you are in a heap of trouble!"

Cavenaugh stood up quickly, stubbing his cigar out in the ashtray. "Mr. Bates, or whoever you are, this bank is not in the practice of releasing money to anyone who comes along and says they are an heir of any deceased. We demand proof as a matter of record here! I'll tell you, just as I told the man earlier, I want proof of death and a will or an order from a judge telling me what to do with the money. The first of you that gets here with that will have the proceeds of the account. I'm sick and tired of the likes of you and that other cowboy coming in here and fighting over money left by some man that may have been, probably was, killed by one of you!" Cavenaugh's eyes had turned from blue to a dark shade of gray.

Richmond knew it was time to leave.

The steps of the bank were almost new and hardly yet polished by boots passing over them. Richmond paused at the foot of the steps and leaned against a post. "Olivia, what the hell do we do now? I've got to think this through."

Olivia was thinking also.

"Richmond, there's one thing we can try, I can try." Her voice sounded as dry as the street in front of her. "Von Chesterfield can probably help. He has a lot of connections. I don't think he can get the money for us, but I think he can see that the account is sealed until a judge's order clears it for you, or you can prove it is yours."

Richmond could see that the thought of going to Chesterfield was not sitting pretty on Olivia's mind. But against his protests, she was trying to make up her own mind. "Mr. Chesterfield has influential friends here. And he was good to me for several years. I think he'll listen, Richmond. If not, what harm can it do? All he can do is say no or refuse to even see me."

Richmond knew not to argue with her. Besides, he had no better plan.

"Of course, Richmond, we must go to his house in a carriage. I can't simply walk up the street like a trollop and knock on the door."

Richmond slowly nodded his head, trying to understand her feelings about returning to the man with whom, as she had phrased it on their first meeting, she had lived intimately for some twelve years. He pulled out his dwindling bills and fingered them.

Olivia pushed the money back toward him. "Richmond, I'm going back in that bank and draw out some of my money. I've been known in Denver for years, and there will be no problem for me to get some cash. We can't be running around Denver as paupers."

She came out a few minutes later with the money. "Find us that carriage, Richmond."

The two of them did feel stylish as they drove through the streets in the hired surrey being drawn by a fancy-looking pinto. Olivia looked around her and appreciated how much Denver had changed from the time she had first seen it many years ago. Where there had been tents and shacks, there were now respectable houses and secure neighborhoods. She fussed with her hair as she gave directions to Richmond for the turns in the streets leading to Chesterfield's house. It lay just on the outside of town. Richmond saw the trees first, before glimpsing the house. The tall elms lined the short lane leading to the house and clustered around the dwelling. The house itself was not imposing. It had a Spanish appearance, with walls of immaculate white stucco and a red tile roof. Its overpowering impression was one of cleanliness and orderliness; the flower beds were neatly manicured; large rosebushes stood among the low-cut junipers and other native plants.

The pinto pulled the surrey into the tiny avenue in front of the house.

"I'll wait for you here, Olivia."

"You'll do no such thing, Richmond Bates. We are both going in there."

"Why should I go in there? I've never seen the man."

"You'll see him now. It's your uncle's money we're trying to protect, isn't it?"

He could think of no argument against that. Leaving the surrey, he almost wished the horse would bolt and he could bolt with it. The thought of seeing a former lover of Olivia's, one who had practically kicked her out of the house when he found another, rankled him.

The door was opened by a small Mexican girl who could not have been more than perhaps eleven or twelve years old. She had great dark eyes but was very shy as she whispered a polite greeting, *"Bueno?"*

She replied to Olivia's question quietly. "The senor and senora live at hotel since they buy it."

"Hotel?"

"Palace Hotel." The girl smiled apologetically, as if somehow the disappointment on Olivia's face could be her fault. "I am sorry, senora."

With murmured thanks, Olivia and Richmond retreated to the surrey.

"How do you like that! He married her and no doubt used her money to buy the Palace Hotel! He wanted it since the first day it was built!" Olivia's fingers were tightened into little fists of rage. "He actually married her! Well, we've no choice. Let's go to the Palace Hotel, Richmond."

Olivia's lips remained set in a tight line all the way to the hotel. Richmond glanced sideways at her frequently when she would make a tiny sigh. He began to wonder if she had been in love with this Chesterfield. Unfamiliar pangs of jealousy began to well up inside of him, and he worried that this woman was beginning to mean a lot more to him than he had intended.

Richmond and Olivia were shown into Mr. Chesterfield's ornate quarters at the hotel. Dark-hued wood was abundant, and the chairs were thick and plush. The square-jawed maid who admitted them offered iced tea, which they both accepted eagerly. Soon footsteps could be heard in the corridor outside. Olivia and Richmond glanced at each other with anxiety. The door opened, and a man of medium height and slightly graying hair and a neatly trimmed beard appeared in the doorway. He had a tailored, expensive look about his clothing. His eyes were hard, blue circles. They stared first at Olivia and then moved to settle on Richmond.

With a curt greeting, he led them into his study and took a seat behind a spacious oak desk. Then he returned his gaze to them. Olivia began to speak quickly and briefly explained the problem, asking only that he help out someway at the bank to see that the account was sealed.

Chesterfield listened quietly, staring at a pencil that he constantly rolled between the thumb and forefingers of both hands. When Olivia had finished her story, he turned; and as if they were not in the room, he stared out the window at a blue sky.

Richmond was not sure whether that was his signal for them to go, but he knew he was not going to be shuffled off that easily. He forced himself to sit still, making a real effort to resist twiddling with his hat as he had a tendency to do when he was nervous.

Chesterfield knew Olivia was impeccably honest. If she said this man was an heir to Forrest Bates's property, he knew she was being truthful. He turned back to them after a few minutes of consideration. Twirling the pencil in his fingers, he paused. Then he slung the pencil across the room and stated to Olivia, "All right, I will intercede to see that Cavenaugh does not release that money to anyone but Bates here after he comes up with the will."

Richmond could hear Olivia release her breath.

Chesterfield continued. "One condition, Olivia. That is that you have no more contact with me and none at all with Mrs. Chesterfield, ever!"

Olivia merely rose graciously and offered her hand to Chesterfield. "You have a deal." She then crossed the room silently with Richmond behind her and marched through the hotel to the surrey outside.

Shannon and his men had ridden hard over an old trail known mostly to Indians and outlaws to reach Denver ahead of Richmond and Olivia. The luck they had in the bank disappointed them, but they were hard men and did not give up easily. They saw no reason why their original plan could not work. If they could get their hands on Richmond and the girl again, they were sure they could convince Richmond to produce the will, wherever it was, and return to the bank better prepared.

When Richmond and Olivia had ridden up to the Palace Hotel, Shannon had been lounging across the street in the shade of the Hardluck Saloon, leaning against the wall with his hat tipped slightly over his face. Soon thereafter, Andy and Juan had joined him. The men had bought new clothing as soon as they had got to town, so they were not seen by Richmond or Olivia as they cautiously watched the couple.

CHAPTER 12

THE sheriff's office was in the middle of town, a small wooden building with bars on the windows, looking just about like all the sheriff's offices Richmond had ever seen. Their trip to the sheriff was brief and initially as fruitless as they had expected. After all, they had no evidence that Forrest had been murdered. And the sheriff was right in his observation that, according to Richmond's own story, another man seemed to have identification that he was Richmond Bates, but that the man standing before the sheriff had nothing but his word and that of his female companion. The sheriff was familiar with Shannon and the kind of company he kept, and he admitted he would like to see him behind bars. But the sheriff had nothing on which to base an arrest.

Discreetly, Olivia slid forward in her chair, placing her hand upon the sheriff's desk. A tiny bit of green showed from underneath her fingers. "Sheriff Bradley, have there been no burglaries, no robberies, no attacks on the citizens of Denver within the last few days?" She silently flicked up a finger to reveal the denomination of the bill underneath. "Given Roy Shannon's reputation, isn't it a possibility that he might at least be a suspect warranting a couple of days in custody during your investigation?" She dropped her finger and left her hand demurely on the sheriff's desk.

The sheriff scratched his nose. "Well, Miss Palmer, perhaps you're right; given the scurrilous nature of the man, he could be a likely suspect in a crime or two around here."

Olivia slid the fifty-dollar bill underneath the blotter on

his desk and stood. With a quick nod and a thank-you, she turned and led the way from the cramped office.

Richmond tried to smother a smile as he followed her.

Returning to the street, Olivia and Richmond found a small café where they could have a meal and make plans. Neither of them had any doubt that they would be watched as long as they were in town, but they felt fairly safe in the company of other people. Nevertheless, Richmond kept an eye out for trouble, and Olivia did as well. He realized now, after having watched Olivia negotiating with Von Chester-field and the sheriff, that Olivia's desire to be dressed cor-rectly when she rode into town had more behind it than a pique of vanity. He was pleased with what she had accom-plished.

They dined on a hearty meal of fried chicken, mashed potatoes with gravy, and black-eyed peas. The two ate in silence for a while. "Well, there's one thing for sure, Olivia. If we start out on the trail, even if Shannon is in jail, his men are going to be right on top of us. I hate to be beholden to you any more than I already am," he said, thinking of the few dollars he had left in his pocket, "but I reckon we'd better find us a cheap place to stay for a couple of days and watch for the Bishops." He added without expression, "If Ike got through to them." After a time, he continued, "In case Ike didn't get through, we've got to have another plan, but danged if I've got one now."

She chewed slowly, thinking quietly. Finally, she nodded her head in agreement. "It's all we can do now, I guess."

The next two days were long ones of waiting and watching. The rooms at the cheap boardinghouse were clean, but were warm and stuffy through the day. Olivia rarely ventured from the wide front porch, where a breeze could usually be felt. She had never remembered it being this hot in Denver so early in the year.

Richmond spent his time roaming the streets warily. Some-times he would go to the stable to check on the horses and to talk with the stable hands. The two of them were friendly and seemed to enjoy the conversations whenever Richmond stopped by. At times, he would catch a glimpse of someone who looked like Shannon or one of his men, but he was never able to be sure. He didn't pursue them. Richmond was aware of his shortcomings with a six-shooter. There had never been much reason on the farm to take time to perfect a quick draw. Now, with a rifle, he would have put himself up against just about anyone, for he had been hunting the woods of Arkansas since he was a kid. And his experiences in the war had quickly taught him that it was as easy to shoot a man as it was an animal when your own life depended upon it. But he knew that in a close-range confrontation, he would most likely end up dead unless he got lucky. Richmond Bates was not a man to gamble with his life, and now he had someone else he felt responsible for too.

He spent many hours sitting on a bench outside the many saloons, watching the people. After much time observing, he found it easy to figure out what a man did for a living just from the clothing he wore. Bib overalls, coupled with a long-sleeved shirt and heavy brogans, usually indicated that the man was a carpenter. Miners could be spotted by the jeans and hobnailed boots that seemed to be their uniform. The most interesting apparel had to be explained to him by one of the locals. He had noticed several men sporting jeans with extraordinarily deep cuffs. When he asked someone sharing the bench outside the saloon, he was amused at the explanation. It seems the men were mule skinners, and the size of the team they drove determined the depth of the cuffs they wore. A mule skinner who drove an eight-horse team was entitled to turn an eight-inch cuff. Likewise, the man who had a six-inch cuff drove a six-horse team.

Then there was the afternoon he saw Madame Fereaux. He was lounging in the shade on a bench outside the Silver Slipper. A miner of perhaps sixty years was stretched out on the bench next to him, emitting low snores from time to time, sleeping off a few, Richmond surmised. The afternoon was warm, and a few flies buzzed around the little piles of dung near the hitching rail. There was not much movement along the street. Then he heard the clop-clop of a lone horse approaching slowly from the south end of the street. Glancing casually in that direction, he saw a woman on horseback emerge into full sunlight from the shade of the trees that graced the street along the small residential section that began a few yards below the Silver Slipper. He felt his stomach churn. Richmond looked upon the most startlingly beautiful woman he had ever seen. She was a woman of olive complexion and dark hair that was pulled back from her face and left to cascade down over her shoulders in an abundance of curls. Richmond glanced swiftly at the horse she rode. He was a magnificent stallion of strange coloring. Richmond quickly noted the pale cream color of his silky coat upon which a purest shade of strawberry spots were blended.

The woman was wearing a riding dress of red velvet that was only a shade darker than the strawberry dapples upon the horse. Richmond hardly noticed the plumed cranberry hat that was perched atop the woman's curls. He did notice that the bodice of the dress was cut low and gave an ample view of the woman's flawless shoulders and the tops of her full breasts. Richmond stood up to get a better view and did not know he was staring so obviously at the woman's breasts, which undulated gently with every movement of the horse.

Richmond did not know the old miner had awakened and sat up until he spoke, "Mighty fine animal, ain't she?"

Richmond spoke automatically, as if in a trance. "Yeah, but it's a stallion."

"Oh, well, yeah, if you're speaking' of the horse."

Richmond heard the grizzled miner chuckling behind him.

"That is Madame Fereaux you're lookin' at, son. Now it's not Madam, mind you. It's rumored that she has scratched men's eyes out for calling her Madam. It is Ma*dame*," he repeated, with a heavy accent on the last syllable. "But don't go gettin' any highfalutin ideas about her. Me and you cain't afford her kind. Jist as well, I guess. She'd prob'ly make a man take a bath and put on clean socks before gittin' near her bed." The old miner, however, had stepped up beside Richmond to enjoy the view.

Richmond drank in the sight of her as a thirsty man gulps a dipperful of spring water.

The woman pulled up across the street in front of a ladies' millinery shop. She dismounted slowly, draped the stallion's reins over the rail, and disappeared inside.

Only then did Richmond's attention return to the stallion, which showed powerful shoulders and haunches and a stocking of the strawberry color on his left hind leg.

When the woman emerged from the shop a few minutes later, carrying a small hatbox, Richmond was drawn like a magnet toward her. As he moved forward, the miner tugged at his sleeve, but Richmond ignored him. With quick strides, he was beside the horse before the woman could retrieve the reins from the rail.

"May I help you with your package, Madame?" He made sure his pronunciation was correct as he reached for the small box the woman carried.

Her dark eyes held an expression of surprise as she looked up at him. "Sir, I thank you for your help." She gave the box to him and, walking to the side of the horse, mounted with agility. "I think I can handle my package now." Her pouty lips widened to flash him a smile as she took the box from him.

Before Richmond could think of anything more to say, she sauntered down the street, pausing a few yards down to look back at him with a smile.

Richmond's legs felt a bit wobbly from the encounter, and he turned toward the saloon, where the miner still stood staring at him with a toothless grin. "That's closer than most of us will ever git to her, I reckon."

Strangely, the encounter with Madame Fereaux brought his thoughts back to Olivia, who, he thought, was probably sitting on the wide front porch fanning herself because of the heat and the flies. He admired her for the way she had acted throughout the last few days, never complaining, always carrying her share of the responsibility, and quick to think and plan. Into his thoughts Madame Fereaux crept again, and he doubted that she would be half as good a companion, and he pushed the thoughts of the velvet dress and bouncy bosom out of his mind. Instead he tried to define in his mind this woman that he knew. The closest he could come was that she was terribly smart in a way only those who had looked after themselves could be; she was aware of things around her and could use good judgment. But he could never get away from the remembrance of her womanly ways, her looks, her smell. He had to cut off his thoughts before they got to the sensation of touch. He knew he had to keep control of his thoughts.

Late in the afternoon, Richmond sauntered down to the stable, eaten up by the stress of inactivity. Squatting in the shade of the barn, he and the two stable hands split a plug of chewing tobacco. One of the hands spat quickly and exclaimed, "I'll be damn, Shorty, look who's comin' into town." He pointed a gnarled finger at a man astride a big dun sauntering up the street.

Shorty let out a slow whistle. "I'll be damn!"

Richmond watched the rider drawing nearer. He was a big man with broad shoulders and a barrel chest. A heavy black beard covered the lower part of his face. He rode by the stable, making no stop but looking their way and waving to them with a shout. "Howdy, boys! See ya' later."

"Must be goin' in to have a little snort before he beds down his horse," Shorty commented.

Richmond was curious at the men's comments about the man's arrival. "Who's that?"

"You don't know who that is?" Shorty queried. "Oh, yeah, I fergot you ain't been in these parts long. That there's Deacon Romine, one of the best gunfighters around. Good man, though. Never kilt nobody that didn't ast fer it." He shot a stream of tobacco juice at a horsefly that had lit on a nearby rock.

"What's a gunfighter doing named Deacon?"

Shorty chomped his tobacco a few times before he launched into the long story. "Well, seems Deacon was a deacon in a regular church—Baptist, I think—somewheres down close to Pueblo. Had hisself a nice little ranch and a fam'ly. He picked the wrong day to go to town oncet, and while he was gone a bunch of outlaws rode in on his wife and twelve-year-old boy. The woman and kid tried to defend theirselves, but the outlaws cut 'em down and stole six or eight of his best horses. Well, Deacon come home just in time to see 'em ride off herdin' his ponies. He didn't go after 'em then, but stopped to see about his wife and kid. But they was dead. The sheriff down that way formed a posse, but they couldn't get close to them outlaws because they had plenty of fine mounts to switch around to when one horse or t'other got tired.

"Well, Deacon warn't too good with a gun back then, but he dropped out of the church, and so I heared, practiced all day long seven days a week for a month or two. Then he hit the road lookin' fer the bunch that kilt his fam'ly. It took him nigh onto six months of lookin' and askin' about the horses, 'cause he didn't know nothin' 'bout the men. Oncet he got on their trail, he stayed on it. They had done more killin' than just his fam'ly. He got 'em eventually. All four of 'em. Got hisself a reputation, too. Now he cain't hardly get a good night's sleep so many of them young squirts think to make their reputation by killin' Deacon. He tries to get by doin' a little prospectin' here and there, but they ain't no peace fer 'im."

The talk seemed all gone out of Shorty as he stopped for several minutes chewing his wad of tobacco. "Good man, Deacon is," he said as he stood up and headed for a customer riding in.

Richmond remained leaning against the wall of the barn for a few minutes, thinking about the deacon and wondering what kind of world he had come to. When the war had ended, he had hoped never to have to use his gun against anything but a squirrel for his supper, or a deer, or maybe an occasional water moccasin. He wondered if the money and the gold were worth it. It would be good to just hit the trail and ride back to Arkansas with Olivia, if she would go with him. But he knew that was not a choice he had any longer. Shannon was still somewhere around, watching and waiting for him to ride out of town. He shaded his eyes and looked toward the hills, although he had just about given up hope that the Bishop brothers would be riding into town.

PART IV

The Ute and the Arapaho

CHAPTER 13

DEACON Romine had never put his gun out for hire, so he hesitated when Richmond made him a proposal in the Silver Slipper the afternoon following his arrival. He studied Richmond's story, and he knew Shannon, Slade, and the two Jicarilla-Mexicans by reputation. Deacon finally named his price, based on a trip to Wells Springs and a safe arrival back in Denver with the will. The two men made brief plans for supplies and extra horses.

Richmond had mixed feelings as he walked back to the boardinghouse to give Olivia the news. In hiring Deacon Romine, he was admitting that something had happened to Ike before or after he reached the Bishops or they would have been here by now. Although he had never met the two young men, he had acquired respect for them through things he had heard of them. It was a temptation to saddle Rowdy and ride away from it all. But he could not walk away from Olivia. The least he could do was to see that Forrest's money would ensure a decent life for her. And he could not let his uncle's killers, if in fact that's what they were, walk away with everything Forrest had acquired.

He looked at a thunderhead building up to the west and wondered if his farmland would get sufficient rain for a good crop this year. The kind of deep homesickness he had not felt since the war rushed through him. He hoped Olivia would be safe in Denver while he was away; perhaps there were former friends with whom she could stay.

When he related his plans to her she jumped up from the porch swing where she had been sitting. "Richmond Bates, I will not stay behind, cooped up here in some little room sipping tea and worrying myself to death! How could you think of such a thing?"

Richmond felt his face growing red, through frustration. "What am I supposed to do, Olivia? Let a woman risk her life out there again? You've been through enough. I might not even be here today if it hadn't been for you!" He could tell by the look on her face as soon as the last words were out of his mouth that he had said the wrong thing.

She seized the opportunity he had so innocently provided. With assurance in her voice obliterating the anger she felt, she spoke quietly. "You're right, Richmond Bates. I just might have saved your life. I doubt it, but I might have. So you owe me the chance to go with you. You know I can hold my own when it comes to trouble. Give me one good reason, just one, why I should not go with you—besides my own safety, and that is my business and my choice."

He knew the argument was over.

The next morning, before sunup they went to the stables to meet Deacon Romine. There were surprises on both sides.

In the morning, Olivia had changed back into her mining clothes and had swept her hair up into a chignon underneath her hat, but there was no mistaking that it was a woman accompanying Richmond Bates as the two of them strode quickly into the stable yard. Deacon was bent over checking out the shoes on one of the extra horses bought for the quick trip. When he saw Richmond approach, he waved to him and looked up from the hoof he was inspecting.

He let the horse's foot drop when he realized Richmond had a woman with him. Nearby, an Indian raised his eyes from where he was packing supplies into saddlebags and let out a slow "Mm-hmm," as he appraised the beauty strolling toward them carrying a rifle and sporting a gun on her hip.

Deacon could tell that this woman was not accompanying Richmond just so she could say good-bye. He wiped his hands on his pants and walked toward Richmond.

Olivia could see the animosity in Deacon's face as he

approached. She glanced beyond him and saw the red-bronze man who kept stashing supplies into saddlebags.

Richmond attempted an introduction. "Deacon, this here's Miss Olivia Palmer, and she'll be riding with us." He, too, could see the disapproval on Deacon's face.

"Not with us, she won't. We don't ride with women."

The Indian looked up from his work.

There was a moment of silence, and Olivia glanced from the heavily bearded white man to the Indian, who was still kneeling on the ground, dressed in buckskin clothing, his hair gathered into long flowing bunches underneath each ear. For a moment, she could imagine him with white war paint smeared around his facial features. She spoke crisply. "Mr. Romine, who do you mean when you say 'We don't ride with women'?"

"I mean me and Two Dogs here. We don't ride with women." He repeated the last for emphasis.

"Mr. Romine, I don't ride with Indians." She emphasized the pronoun.

"Well, if I ride out of here, Two Dogs is goin' to be along." He looked toward Richmond. "We heard last night that there is some Ute moving through south of here, maybe some Arapaho, too."

Olivia was not going to let the focus of the argument go astray. "If any of this party heads out, I will be with them."

Richmond was caught in the middle. "Deacon Romine, Miss Palmer's right. That money I gave you to buy horses and supplies with . . . well, that was her money. I guess she has a right to go if she wants to. She's darn good with that rifle and won't get in anybody's way." He wished Olivia could be happy fanning herself on the front porch while he got this business out of the way, but her standing up to Deacon Romine gave him a strange sense of pride.

Olivia knew she had to relent and let the Indian accompany them, although the idea of being overcome by savages almost sent her storming back to the boardinghouse. "Then

I guess it's all settled." She strode toward Carly with a stern look on her face. She missed the humorous expression on Two Dogs' face.

Two Dogs finished his business of packing and started slinging the gear on the animals. Deacon relented.

The rather unsettled group started out just as the sky was beginning to take on a rich golden color. Each of them felt certain that their every move was being watched. Shortly outside of town they took to the cover of the trees, hoping to evade any pursuers or at least to make themselves more difficult targets. Everyone except Two Dogs had an extra horse. The Kiowa had refused to be hampered by another animal, having faith in the lasting power of his big stallion for long, swift flight if necessary.

It was near noon before the big clouds started forming overhead. When the lightning started flashing, Olivia felt the electricity all around. Her horse tried to bolt when a lightning flash hit a big pine some seventy-five yards away. She reined Carly up until he could get his mind set on the trail again. He finally began to follow Deacon's dun. His ears were alert, and his mind absorbed by the flashes in the sky and the noise of thunder.

The trees they passed through were wet and clingy things. Leaves stuck to saddles, clothing, and hair as they skirted a stand of elm. Among the pines, large cones rained down, and the saddles gathered sticky puddles of resin. Olivia watched the dun ahead, and out of the corner of her eye caught glimpses of Richmond astride Rowdy behind her.

Olivia was not well prepared when the dun's hooves bit into the ground ahead of her and sent mud flying. She only knew to kick Carly's sides and get him moving; from what or toward what, she didn't yet know. She found out soon enough. As Carly raced along keeping close on the heels of the dun, the forest was alive with Indians, racing from behind trees. Olivia expected shouts and yells, but the assault was being carried out silently, which made it even more frightening. An Indian in buckskin leaped between her and Deacon's horse. He reached for Carly's bridle. The big horse reared, striking the Indian in the chest. Olivia could feel the sickening crunch of bone beneath Carly's hooves. Her horse turned slightly aside and found his own clearing through the trees.

Lightning danced around, thunder crashed close by, and Carly continued to run. Olivia let him have his head and clung to the saddle and the reins. She heard shots behind her, but she continued to let the horse run, praying he did not step into a rabbit's burrow and break a leg. Big raindrops began to pelt the horse's sides, and he still ran as if pursued by Satan. Olivia had lost any sound of the battle behind her. She felt totally alone rushing through country that had turned out to be a long mesa. The trees were behind her, and she could only assume that Richmond, Deacon, and the Kiowa were nowhere around.

She had no idea that the mesa was a dead end. Only when Carly pulled up, snorting and breathing hard, did she realize the way off the mesa was a sheer drop of maybe five hundred feet. The lightning-shattered daylight glistened on the waters down below where the river made its way through sandstone cliffs. She felt her heart pounding as if she had been doing the running instead of Carly. Looking about, she finally realized she was alone except for the Indians rapidly approaching.

She felt herself a fool as she heard hooves of Indian horses pounding the earth. There was no place to hide or run. The rain continued to fall hard, making a veil between her and the Indians. In panic, she reached toward her rifle, but just as quickly pulled her hand back. She could think of nothing to do except watch them coming toward her in a rush; firing at them would be a deadly mistake. She felt helpless.

She saw a man propelling himself at her and felt the thud as her body fell upon the wet clay of the mesa. The Indian was upon her, holding down her hands. She tried struggling and kicking, but the man was strong. As quickly as the attack had come, it was over. Panting heavily from exertion and excitement, Olivia reached up to push her hair back. The chignon had come loose, and the mass of blond hair piled over her face. She realized the Indian who had jumped at her had turned her loose quickly.

The Indian stood staring at her as if he were a bronze statue cast permanently with a look of amazement upon his face. There were two companions with him; each shared a similar look of astonishment. They began to look from her to one another. The one who had attacked her found his voice. "Woman! Small woman! Fight big!"

At that time, Olivia became aware of a rider on a black pony with white spots approaching them with three braves behind him. When the three assessed the situation, they began laughing and chattering in their language, obviously poking fun at their companions. The rider on the spotted pony did not join in the laughter and banter. Olivia felt he must be the leader from his somber expression and the regal air he carried. With a cold look, he cut off the laughter of the others. He made a swift motion with his left hand that made her flinch, but he added, "Go get your horse."

It took a few minutes to gather Carly and to calm him so that she could mount. The seven Indians sat on their horses and watched. Olivia wondered about the shots that had been fired after Carly bolted away from her companions. She wondered what had happened to them, but she was not given a chance to ask. As soon as she was mounted, the Indians formed a loose circle around her and galloped back the way from which they had come. Olivia was fearful that if Richmond, Deacon, and the Kiowa were still alive they would appear on the trail riding toward them, and she knew the three would be no match on the open mesa for her seven captors.

Soon, though, she and the Indians were headed down a steep embankment that had been hidden so tightly behind a stand of juniper that she would never have seen it. The tiny path led down the west side of the mesa. The rain had stopped, but it was still dangerously slippery on the way down. A weak sun came through the clouds, drying Olivia's wet clothing and caking the mud on her khakis and shirt. Her jacket was still tied behind Carly's saddle and was free from mud, though somewhat damp.

The group descended single-file, with Carly plodding along behind the Indian mount in front of him. Olivia began to wonder about the nature of the men she rode with. They wore no war paint, and she doubted that they were murdering renegades, else she would probably be seeing the scalps of Richmond, Deacon Romine, and Two Dogs dangling from the black and white pony that the leader rode. Perhaps hers might even be hanging alongside, she thought with a chill. Still, she had no assurance that her traveling companions were alive and well after the Indian attack.

Each of the Indians was young, with only the leader being perhaps near middle age, and each rode with grace and a certain proud defiance. The man on the spotted pony led the way down the steep hillside. Olivia looked at him searchingly when the horses and men between them thinned out in different directions so that she could see him well. He sat squarely upon the horse, which wore nothing but a saddle blanket and a bridle fashioned from strong-looking bands of leather. The man wore scarcely more than his horse, only a pair of leather britches and moccasins, both of which looked well-made to Olivia. A scar across his left shoulder had mended into little gathered puckerings of flesh that zigzagged down from the edge of his shoulder to a spot midway on his back.

Olivia's mind was haunted by the death of her family at the hands of Indians when she was a girl, and stories of horrible mutilations and killings came back to her. She struggled to remember the details of recent unrest among the Indians that had led to many of them leaving the reservations. Perhaps somewhere nearby this group had a camp where there were families. The hard-riding renegades never chose to burden themselves with women or children when they were on a rampage, she knew, unless it was a white woman whom they could use for sport and then adorn their lodge with her hair. For once, Olivia wished her hair was a true black or dark brown, because it was rumored that Indians favored long, blond scalps.

They continued to ride the rest of the day at a quick pace, varying their speeds to cover the maximum number of miles while not wearing out the horses. Every mile of Carly's familiar stride gave Olivia more confidence. Her breathing slowed, and her mind began to function more reasonably. Night brought them to a meadow tightly ringed by hills, a place where a small fire and a little smoke would not be easily detected by any others in the area. Water was plentiful, and Olivia had to avert her eyes when men stripped to wash themselves in the stream that ran through the meadow.

The Indians saw that she had food, water, a blanket; and then she was staked out in the middle of the camp to a pole thrust firmly into the ground, her ankle tied to the pole with a rawhide thong. Moment by moment, she endured the dark hours, wondering what had happened to Richmond, Deacon, and the Indian.

Sometimes, she bitterly wanted to think that Two Dogs might be a part of some plan with her captors, but in thinking it through she had to admit she could not blame Two Dogs. He had not had any idea she was to be traveling with them any sooner than she had realized he would be traveling with them.

Before morning, she finally fell asleep and dreamed of the leering expression she had seen more than once on Roy Shannon's face. It almost made her glad to be in the company of the Indians when she awoke from her nightmare.

The next day, they continued to travel westward at a grueling speed across mountains higher than Olivia had ever crossed before. It seemed to her they were headed west, but in a slightly northerly direction. The Indians seemed indifferent to her, but she knew they kept an eye on her constantly. Olivia watched the back trail over her shoulder, seeking strange rock formations, unusual trees, anything in the way of a landmark that would point the way back for her when she escaped.

The constant tension and the hard pace were difficult. At some point midway through the day, Olivia felt herself growing weak and her stomach beginning contortions. With embarrassment, she finally got the attention of the Indian riding nearest. With gestures pointing toward the bushes and toward her stomach, she got her message across. A shout from the nearest Indian brought the riders to a halt, and Olivia bounded off Carly, hitting the bushes none too soon. She was retching into the grass at once. When her stomach settled a little, she wiped the vomit off her chin with the back of her hand, and felt incensed at this indignity.

Turning from the bushes, she walked toward the waiting Indians. She approached the black and white horse.

"You on the spotted pony! I want to know where you are taking me and why!" She was surprised at the forcefulness of her voice and that she had spoken up at all. A blind fury made her indifferent as to the outcome of her boldness.

The rider of the spotted pony looked pointedly at her. "I am Half-Moon Bear of the Ute. Woman does not talk. Ride." He motioned for her to get back on her horse.

"This woman will talk, Half-Moon Bear, or whoever you are. You might as well kill me here as somewhere down the road, if that is your plan. I want to know why you keep me and where we are going."

Half-Moon Bear studied her for a moment. "We want your horse and the horses of your friends. Guns, maybe. We hold you for horses and maybe guns."

"My friends, as you call them, may never come. I have

known one of them maybe two weeks, a half-moon. The other two I met but four hours before you kidnapped me, and one of them was an Indian, probably in cahoots with you and your braves!" Her eyes glistened with fire, and her words frightened her, but she was sick at heart and brazened by her anger.

CHAPTER 14

RICHMOND was never quite sure when he lost sight of Olivia. The Indians created a mass of confusion when they appeared, seemingly from nowhere, slashing with knives, and a couple, perhaps three, firing pistols. Richmond managed to see Carly running through the trees. Before he could go in pursuit, he felt a vicious slash across his upper left arm and turned to fire toward an attacking brave. He missed and cursed himself for not having had his rifle across his saddle. Deacon had his handgun firing rapidly, but the darting Indians made poor targets. The fight was short. Suddenly, a bloodcurdling wail came from their back trail, and the quick booming of Two Dogs's Henry raged through the trees. The Kiowa came rushing in sounding like a dozen blood-crazed warriors. The Indians disappeared almost as quickly as they had arrived, pulling two injured men with them.

The silence was thick when the Indians were out of sight. "Let's clear out of here fast before they get a notion to come back," Deacon said.

Other than the quick slice to Richmond's upper arm, which was bleeding only moderately, none of the men had been injured. A couple of the horses had minor nicks on their shoulders and flanks. Both Richmond and Deacon had seen the way Olivia had gone, so they took off in that direction, quickly at first, then slowing as Two Dogs looked for sign along the sometimes rocky and hard-packed surface over which they traveled, seeking out Carly's prints from among those of unshod Indian horses.

Over the years, much of Deacon's religious discipline had

been eroded, and he was soon cursing. "Now, dammit, we've got to watch our back trail for Shannon, while we're trying to follow a bunch of damned redskins."

Soon Deacon had a sickening feeling in his stomach. He could tell that Olivia's horse had headed toward the dead-end mesa. He waited for a while to be sure before he told Richmond. When he pulled up for a few minutes to explain what he suspected, Richmond's questions burst forth.

"Simmer down, Richmond. I'll give you the whole story as best I see it. Those were Utes back there that attacked us. They're not usually warring against whites these days, especially not this far east. But the gover'ment has riled them up, trying to get back some of the lands they had reserved for the Utes. Not that the danged redskins want to live on it. They just don't want the whites to get it back. My guess is that this is a hunting party. If it wasn't, they would've tried harder to get our scalps. But even a huntin' party won't pass up a good horse like the woman rode." He omitted to say they wouldn't pass up a good-looking woman like Olivia, either. "I think we can be sure the Utes have her by now. I think she'll be safe for a while. There's a way down that mesa. Two Dogs can find it." He urged his horse forward. "At least if we're traveling close to a bunch of Utes, it might make Shannon think a good long time before they start gunnin' up the country around us."

The men continued to follow the trail, rifles over the front of their saddles. It was not long before the prints on the ground confirmed Deacon's thoughts. The Indians had not even made an effort to conceal their tracks; even if they had, the rainstorm would have frustrated their efforts. The three made their way down the narrow pathway, fighting an early darkness underneath clouds that seemed to be promising more rain.

Their camp that night was dark. Supper was jerked beef and biscuits and a long drink of cool water. They had found a fresh spring and good grass for the horses. Through the darkening afternoon, they had trailed the Utes, knowing the Indians were only an hour or so ahead of them. The Kiowa had found fresh tracks of unshod ponies riding parallel to the trail of the Utes, a little more than a mile away. The three hung back, not sure what to expect. The parallel trail had Two Dogs puzzled, so as the sky became a mass of stars and dim moonlight, he faded out of camp. Long before daylight, he was back, saying nothing to either man until morning.

"Arapaho," the Kiowa declared over coffee. They had risked a small fire to boil coffee and completed their meal with more jerky and a few stale biscuits.

The two white men waited for Two Dogs to continue.

"Not a war party, probably just looking for horses." Two Dogs motioned toward their stock. "We keep good eye on them. The Arapaho know we are here. They scouted our camp through the night."

Richmond had difficulty accepting the situation with the stoicism that the Kiowa showed. The Arapaho had been sneaking about their camp through the night; a party of Utes ahead of them with a captive; and Roy Shannon somewhere behind them. He thought of the farm he had left in early spring, where the only worry he would have this time of the year would be whether rain would come at the right time to make a good crop.

"Couldn't we just give the damned horses to somebody and get this over with?" He stared at Deacon.

"It don't work that way with Indians. We'll watch. Keep your rifle handy."

Richmond pulled his Winchester closer and checked again to be sure it was loaded.

That day, in spite of Richmond's impatience, they hung back, merely taking direction from the trail of the Ute horses. Two Dogs rode out and returned midday to report that the Arapaho were still traveling along in the same direction on the opposite side of the ridge of mountains to the left. Richmond felt an urge to go riding into the midst of the

Utes, but he knew that it would be suicide, so he decided to give Deacon and Two Dogs a little more time.

Sensing Richmond's restlessness, Deacon spoke to him. "I think I can set your mind at ease a little about the Ute. They undoubtedly know we are behind. They want our horses, possibly our guns, but they want to get back to where their camp is. The Ute have been a little shy of horses and guns since they've been wrestlin' with the gover'ment as to whether they're gonna stay on their reservations or not. The Arapaho are in a little better position; nobody's rounded up enough of them at one time to even try to get them onto a reservation. But they are the horse-stealingest tribe I know of.

"Now the Utes and the Arapaho are kind of baitin' each other. The Arapaho want to wait until the Utes get closer to their camp, where there will be enough horses to make a raid worthwhile. The Utes want to get back closer to more of their braves and in the meanwhile are waiting to see if anything happens in their favor. Trying to outguess the patience of Indians can make you old before you know it, Richmond. Now, the Arapaho know our horses are not likely to increase in number, so they'll just bide their time. None of them really want our scalps, else we wouldn't have them by now, and the same is true for Miss Olivia."

It was not often that Deacon Romine spoke much, but when he did, it was usually at length and carried answers to all the questions that a man could think of. He seemed to Richmond to be a man of hard inner core with the ability to perceive and assimilate all that happened around him. Richmond knew nothing to do but put his faith in Deacon and Two Dogs for now.

After the first night, they figured both groups of Indians knew of their presence, which meant they had to keep their senses even more alert for trouble but they could once again enjoy their mealtimes. Night camps were still fireless, but they made use of a fire to cook their evening meal alongside some stream, then moved on to bed down in a dry camp with their backs against a cliff or boulders high enough to ward off an unexpected attack. Mornings brought a hot meal and strong coffee, when they no longer felt the need to hide. Many times Richmond would get an eerie feeling that someone was watching him. When he mentioned this to Deacon, the man replied, "Well, you're becoming a western man, Bates. If you get the feelin' that somebody is watchin' you, somebody probably is. Now just learn to find where he's hiding and who he is." He rode on twisting a chew off a plug of tobacco. "That feelin' has kept me alive many's the time."

The Kiowa brought regular reports on what was happening around them with the Indians; and they knew if Shannon tried to surprise them, he would probably be surprised himself. To Richmond, it seemed impossible that one Kiowa scout could keep up with so much around; he finally figured out the scout probably swapped information with other Indians from the Ute and Arapaho tribes.

Finally, Two Dogs made a declaration. "I know the leader of the Utes."

Of course, Richmond and Deacon had figured out from the beginning that Two Dogs had known who was leading the band of Indians. They had also known that the Kiowa would take his time in telling them anything about the man.

"The leader is Half-Moon Bear. He is a good warrior and good hunter. Walks with honor among his people."

Deacon didn't know if Richmond understood enough about Indian values and customs to realize that a man who "walks with honor among his people" would be apt to slip up behind you and slit your throat if you were not of his people, just as he would kill a rattlesnake or grizzly in his path.

"Half-Moon Bear, huh? Well, Richmond, that makes things a little clearer. I've heard many times about the man. One of the main things is that he likes good horses; no doubt he was the one riding that fine spotted pony back there where we got ambushed." Knowing Half-Moon Bear was the leader shed some light on things.

"Richmond, the Ute have been restless the last couple, three, maybe four years, what with their idea that the gover'-ment has been tryin' to cheat them on their lands, like I'd said before. I think the Ute are lettin' us trail along to get us near enough to their people that they can surround us with enough warriors that even our repeating rifles will stand no chance. They're leading us into a trap. Then again, the Ute and Arapaho might be together in this, planning to split up our horses and guns between the two camps. Who can figure out Indians for sure? We've got six good horses, Bates. Is the woman more important? I'm not sure if we can get out of here with both, and maybe not either. Seems like for us, we'd been lucky if Shannon had just ambushed us somewhere." Deacon was thinking that he had taken on a lot more than he had bargained for in Denver. But then he thought of the loss of his family and knew Bates was making the right decision. He hoped he could spare the younger man any reason for feeling the need for vengeance that had eaten him for the last few years. "Of course," Deacon continued, "we might be able to trade some of the horses for the woman. Just possible, wouldn't give you odds on that."

The next report from the Kiowa in the morning was not good. He rode into camp just as the fire was ready for cooking. Richmond had found an early-morning squirrel, which he brought down quickly with his rifle. A dab of flour and a little lard enabled him to make a concoction of fried squirrel and wild onion, which would have tempted any of the Indians who happened to be within smelling distance. The Kiowa's announcement was simple: "About two hours behind us, four white men."

During the night, Richmond had been mulling over the possible outcome of every war maneuver and stance that might work in this situation. He had his mind made up a few minutes after Two Dogs had finished speaking. Richmond stared long and thoughtfully at a place in the Colorado sky where spires stood near the trail they were taking. He had watched the spires since daylight, wary of an attack from the grassy knoll that rolled between them. Now they took on another significance. He pointed in that direction. "Know what's up there, either of you?"

Two Dogs spoke first. "Water there. Good sight of country."

Deacon also responded. "Ain't been there. What's on your mind?" He thought he knew, but he wanted to ask anyway.

The spires stood on the base of a grassy mesa high above the trail the men were following. The rocky columns pointed magnificently toward the sky.

"Any protection up there, Two Dogs?"

"Small cave, maybe six feet into mountainside. Plenty trees."

Richmond fell quiet, thinking hard about the Indians around and Shannon behind.

After they had finished their breakfast and scraped their tin plates and rinsed them, Richmond had a quick conversation with Deacon and Two Dogs. Both men began to nod their heads as Richmond spoke. Then they tightened the girths on their saddles and rode. Two dogs knew a way to the top of the spires from the west side. Shannon and his men would be following a trail from the east and would have no way of knowing that the three were hidden up above them as they passed the spires.

The morning sun was shining well into the valley as the three lay with their rifles among the rocks, carefully watching the trail below. Their horses were tethered among brush that grew at the back of the small mesa. It was not a long wait until the four horsemen they had been expecting rode into sight.

The four stopped just below. The man called Poncho got off his horse and studied the place where Bates, Romine, and Two Dogs had cooked their morning meal. Poncho's right arm was motioning toward the west when the bullet from Richmond's gun hit the dirt beside him. Quickly other bullets pelted around the four, and they ran for cover in the young grove of sugar pine, just as Richmond had expected them to do. A steady rain of fire played around their hideaway, keeping them trapped. There were clear open spaces all around, and Shannon's men could go nowhere without being seen from up above. Firing held them effectively in the trap.

If death had been the hand Bates and Deacon had wanted to deal, it would have been easy. The young trees in the thicket did not offer complete concealment. They could easily see that Andy had moved toward the back of the grove leading the horses, making a rippling movement in the branches and tops of the young pines. At a signal from Deacon, Two Dogs slipped down the western slope below the spires. An hour later, amid heavy gunfire from above pinning the band below in their scanty cover, the Kiowa herded their four horses out of the small grove. A shriek from Two Dogs had surprised both the horses and the men within the trees as the Kiowa swung onto the back of Poncho's powerful brown horse. Clinging low over the horse's neck, the Kiowa screeched and shouted, making the other horses bolt toward the clearing. Richmond thought the screams of the Kiowa were surely heard by the Ute and Arapaho within the area, perhaps by the entire Ute and Arapaho nations. He grinned at the thought. Richmond kept peppering the countryside below as he watched Two Dogs crouched on the brown horse, expertly blending in with the animal and herding the others straight toward the western slope that led to the mesa.

Richmond, Deacon, and Two Dogs waited out the rest of the day impatiently. It was tempting to ride on or to cut down the four with rifle fire. But Richmond stuck to his plan. It took only an occasional sprinkle of bullets to keep the men among the trees. The horses Two Dogs had run out had their saddles on them, but the men below had retained the presence of mind to remove their canteens and saddlebags when the shooting started, so they had food and extra ammunition.

The coals were still glowing in the campfire and Richmond sat brushing his teeth with a small twig trimmed from a cottonwood when the Kiowa slipped out of camp quietly. Richmond quit sucking the twig to keep an eye toward the encampment below.

It was close to midnight when the Kiowa gave his birdcall and strode into camp carrying three pairs of boots strapped together. Two Dogs rarely smiled, but now his teeth could be seen in the dim light of the fire as he held the boots of the three men in his hand. "Other man wore boots," he said as he held up his knife indicating he had done away with the one who had guarded the camp.

Although he said nothing about his adornment, around Two Dogs's neck was a leather thong that had not been there earlier. From the thong dangled two ears still bloodied about the base.

"Well, we can figure on Shannon being slowed down a little. It'll be hard, traveling out here with no horses, no boots, and one less man, but I wouldn't stake anything on it being over with them. I've a feeling they've been through worse before." Richmond was trying to get his thoughts together.

"Bates, I should've stuck to it," said Deacon.

"What are you talking about? Stuck to what?"

"My decision not to ride with a woman. I should never have done it!"

"Then we wouldn't have ridden at all. That's all there is to it."

Two Dogs turned away so that they would not see his smile. From the first, he had known he would just as soon ride with the woman as with most of the men he had shared the trail with over the years.

CHAPTER 15

THE next morning they broke camp early under a starry sky. There was no coffee or bacon this morning. The risks were too great. Three men with a herd of ten good horses could be too much of a temptation to even the most peaceful Arapaho or Ute. At least they could quit worrying about Shannon for now. The stirrups of the saddles on the new horses had been tied up to keep from spooking the horses as they made a fast ride. The saddles might be extra baggage or might be useful for bargaining later.

Richmond had to depend on Two Dogs's feeling as to where the Ute encampment lay, and to hope that the Indian was right when he said a day's hard ride would lead them into the camp ahead of Half-Moon Bear's party. It was important to ride in boldly before Half-Moon Bear and his party arrived. A show of courage was an important part of their strategy. Their options were few at this point.

Late that afternoon, near sundown, Deacon and Two Dogs crept up to a brushy atoll overlooking a small hidden valley. Two Dogs had been right; the Ute camp was below. They searched visually through the camp, taking stock of the inhabitants. They saw no more than fifteen or so braves and several women with children about. As Two Dogs had expected, this seemed to be a hunting and foraging expedition, with the women along to dig for roots, gather medicinal herbs, and clean and preserve meat and hides.

They prepared to ride in, knowing it unlikely that their presence had not been marked by guards. "Well, they ain't nothin' an Indian respects more than bravery and horses. Let's show 'em we got both." Deacon was ready to go.

The three rode with their string of horses to a high point overlooking the Indian camp. They approached slowly, ambling along in a relaxed manner, looking like a group of horse traders. The saddles on the extra mounts had been stashed in a thick stand of brush to increase their chances of looking like regular traders.

Two braves soon rode out to meet them. They pulled up and watched as the white men and the Kiowa moved the horses toward them. Deacon rode ahead to meet the Indians. He returned soon, looking successful. "They say we can camp over yonder, under them cottonwoods." He added under his breath, "The horses surely won't be taken by the thievin' Arapaho while we're in a Ute camp."

Richmond did not feel the security that Deacon and the Kiowa seemed to feel, but he knew as long as they were accepted at the Ute camp at least their scalps were safe. Once out of the camp, what happened could be anybody's guess. The men established their camp underneath the nearby cottonwoods, along the same side of the small creek that ran through the Ute camp.

Just as the moon began to light the darkened sky, there was a disturbance.

"A mite of running over there," Deacon proclaimed as he sat up from his blankets and began to pull on his boots. Richmond had already risen and stood watching over toward the Ute camp. He saw several riders coming through the small pass to the south. Glancing toward the fires, he could see the women building them up and braves running out to meet the riders. Richmond felt his throat muscles tighten, and he felt a restraining hand on his arm. It was Deacon. "It must be her, Bates. But don't lose control of yourself and go running into their midst."

The two men stood in the shadows and watched. Their attention first focused on the woman with the yellow hair who rode in bound at the wrists. She sat straight on her horse. Richmond was too far away to see her eyes, but he would have guessed they were wide with terror at being in the midst of an Indian camp. Half-Moon Bear rode majestically. Shortly before riding into camp, he made a sign toward one of his braves and toward Olivia. The young brave reached for Carly's bridle and led him toward a large tepee. A woman with graying blond hair met the two at the fire in front of the tepee. Richmond and Deacon could see the white woman helping Olivia from her horse after the brave had untied her hands. The two men could see that Olivia was rather unsteady when her boots hit the ground, but they had both experienced the same sensation after a long day in the saddle. All their peering could not tell them whether physical harm had come to Olivia.

Olivia's attention picked up as they rode into the Ute camp. Her thoughts of escape had been put aside in favor of thoughts of survival for now. The hours she had been forced up and down the mountains, sometimes without water for hours at a time, made her grateful to see the firelight coming from the Ute camp. It might mean rest was near. Even in her state of mind, she was sure that Half-Moon Bear calculated her endurance and strained it to what he thought her limits would be. For that reason she had feigned sickness through the day, moaning for her hands to be untied and wretching from time to time as if she suffered from dry heaves. She saved herself as much as possible by pretending weakness.

She was surprised to see the aging white woman there to help her off her horse, but she knew before long that although the woman had the features and coloring of a white woman, she seemed to be Indian throughout. Olivia allowed the woman to lead her inside the tepee and tuck her into a comfortable bed on the ground. Any bed would have been comfortable after her endless hours on the horse. Olivia had no idea she had friends in the Ute camp. She fell deeply asleep after the woman had brought her some warm broth.

Olivia awakened the next morning to the light aroma of a

tea of herbs she could not name. The white woman she remembered from the night before stirred the mixture and held it out to Olivia.

"Thank you. Could I have water, please?" Olivia's lips felt parched. She alternated sips of the tea and deep swallows of water. She and the woman eyed each other for a few minutes while Olivia drank.

"I am White Dove," the woman soon declared. Her voice was soft and pleasing. "There is water here for your bath, and I have brought you fresh clothing."

Olivia sat up eagerly, for her body felt sticky and unclean, and she wondered from time to time if she actually could smell herself. White Dove offered her a small square of red cloth similar in texture to the calico skirts she had seen Indian women wear. Eagerly, she plunged the cloth into the basin expecting to have a refreshing, warm bath. Instead the water was icy cold. She made up her mind to say nothing as she swished her hands around in the pottery vessel for a few moments. Using a sudsy, soaplike mixture, which White Dove explained came from the root of the yucca plant, Olivia bathed, surprised at how quickly she became used to the cold water and how refreshed she felt afterward.

Her face lit up when she saw the clothing White Dove offered to her. They were soft buckskin trousers and a long top. Olivia felt the clothes, loving the softness, admiring the small stitches of something that looked like animal sinew and the delicate fringe that ran down the side seams of the lower garment and around the bottom of the shirt. When she slipped into them, the clothing felt soft and easy to wear.

After she was dressed, White Dove left her alone for a few moments while she removed the bath water. Olivia looked at the sky, showing a brilliant blue through the small smoke hole above, and listened to the sounds of people outside. She wanted to be outside too, feeling the warmth of the sun and the cool morning breezes. She stepped just outside the tepee and watched the stirrings among the people in the camp.

Smoke was rising from the morning fires. Most of the people about were men, but a few women were working around the cooking fires and tending a child here and there. One woman was already seriously at work, scraping a deer hide with some instrument that looked like a long blade of bone honed to a sharpness along one edge. Letting her eyes roam around the camp, she saw that the countryside seemed peaceful, the creek filled with dark, rapidly flowing water, the dark green of the pine and spruce contrasting with the tender green of the grasses. Her eyes searched among the Indian horses in a small corral nearby. She felt better when she saw Carly grazing in luxuriant grass. Turning toward the west, she saw another small camp where smoke curled from a low fire. There were horses tethered nearby. Involuntarily, she took a small step forward when she realized one of them was Rowdy.

The figures around the fire were in shadow, but suddenly one sprang up and seemed to be looking in her direction. She could tell at this distance only that it was a white man, but she held her breath and took a few slow steps. Before she could go farther, White Dove grabbed her left elbow and gently turned her back toward the tepee. Olivia struggled to get her arm from the woman's grasp. "No! I want to be outside in the sunshine!"

White Dove's grasp was strong. "No, maybe later. Now you should rest. You are still tired." She led Olivia firmly back inside the tepee.

Olivia decided it was best if she went in and sat down. She wanted to question White Dove about the men camped nearby, but she decided to wait until she could act more casual about it.

Richmond had stood up sharply when he caught a glimpse of Olivia as she stared his way. Deacon followed his gaze just in time to see her being propelled back inside by the white woman. They glanced at each other.

"Hold on, Richmond. I'm sure Half-Moon Bear will invite us in soon to talk."

The invitation came before long. A woman was sent with a message to them to share a meal with Half-Moon Bear.

Half-Moon Bear was an imposing figure as he stood watching the two white men pace toward him. He wore no ornaments around his neck or his arms, and was clothed only in trousers and moccasins. His naked torso had been covered with an ointment, making it glisten in the sun, accenting his muscular build. He was a mature man, but one who still retained prime strength. His long hair was pulled back underneath each ear and was secured with some sort of bone restrainers. He stood flanked on either side by braves, younger but not nearly as imposing in stature and bearing.

The meal was a simple one of roasted venison, some sort of herbal soup, and a mush made from ground piñon nuts from the last harvest season. Half-Moon Bear had a good knowledge of the white man's language. There was much talk of game, the scarcity of buffalo, the abundance of deer and elk in the mountains around them. The meal droned on with no mention of Olivia being made. Richmond's hips soon began to go numb from his immobile position on the grass. Deacon had previously warned Richmond that he did not want to risk their bargaining power by seeming overly eager to ask about the woman. They had both observed the graying white woman moving about the Ute camp and could see from the size of the tepee in which she stayed that she was a respected member of the tribe. This had reinforced Deacon's unspoken concern that a white woman might be more important to them than the horses the Indians coveted.

When Deacon finally got around to mentioning casually that they had noticed that Half-Moon Bear's men had brought in a white woman the night before, Half-Moon Bear looked indifferent. "Yes, she is resting now. Woman was half dead with exhaustion. It is bad." He gave no sign of knowing the woman was from their party.

Nor did Richmond or the Deacon give any sign that their trails had crossed previously either. There would be a time for that, but not now.

Deacon quickly changed to another subject. "If Half-Moon Bear does not object, we will stay here two, three more days and let our horses graze and rest."

Half-Moon Bear indicated his agreement. "Where do you take horses?" His question was asked with seeming ignorance as to where they had got the horses or what they planned to do with them.

Deacon answered as simply and evasively. "They are for trade." He did not say where or for what, for he knew to deal with an Indian in any manner except in battle was to play a game of patience and parlaying. Now was the time for patience. Parlaying would begin when Half-Moon Bear felt he had worn their forbearance down somewhat.

The time they spent camped near the Ute was not unpleasant. There were meals and conversations with Half-Moon Bear and his companions, Horse Standing and Lonely Wolf. Richmond reflected on the Indian custom of naming an individual to reflect some aspect of personality or situation in life, and each time he felt more strongly that Lonely Wolf had been named in error, for he made the tedious time of waiting also a time of entertainment. Lonely Wolf loved to gather the children of the camp around him for stories. For storytime, even the women would stop their chatter as they scraped deer or rabbit hides and listen to Lonely Wolf. A few of the braves gathered, bringing with them the bridles, moccasins, or other goods they might be repairing. Even the Kiowa slipped in quietly and sat nearby to listen, attracting the eyes of all the children with the thong around his neck from which dangled the human ears, which had been dried in the sun and smoked over the campfire to prevent any odor.

Lonely Wolf would tug on the ends of his long braids as he moved dramatically into the stories, speaking a mixture of the Ute language and the white man's so that everyone present could follow the stories. Occasionally, he would rise and act out a portion of the story to mimic stalking a deer, wrestling a bear, or running a spear through a dangerous enemy. When he spoke of the chase, the hunt, or of warfare, his voice was excited, yet melodious, ranging in pitch according to the degree of suspense involved. When he spoke of the agonies endured by the various Indian nations when they were deprived of their homelands and placed upon reservations, his voice became sonorous and firm.

Sometimes when the stories ended and the crowd dispersed back to their other activities, Lonely Wolf, Half-Moon Bear, and Horse Standing would sit alone with the white men, and Lonely Wolf would draw out of Richmond stories of his experiences in the war. A look of polite disbelief would overcome his aging face when Richmond described the great plantations he had encountered as a captain leading his troops through the South. Lonely Wolf would hang his head over stories of slavery and often repeat, "So they would do to my people."

Soon, Deacon became more daring in opening the conversation to the subject of Olivia. "We see the white woman is alive and recovering," he declared one late afternoon.

Half-Moon Bear replied solemnly, "Yes, White Dove takes good care of sick." He paused. "Soon the white woman will be able to endure a ride back to our lodges."

Deacon knew that the main lodges lay to the north over rough, mountainous terrain. "You think she can make it? White women are weak, you know." Deacon began at once to strengthen his bargaining position.

"She can make it."

Deacon chose the truth, flavored with a little bit of deceit. "We have known this woman for some time. She belonged to the brother of the father of this man." He motioned toward Richmond. "You do not want her in your camp. Each month she is doubled over with pains from the woman's curse. The bread she bakes would threaten every tooth in your head. No one can ruin a piece of buffalo meat or deer as quickly as the woman you hold. The one thing she does well is ride horses. She would probably steal many horses away from Half-Moon Bear after she had ruined his stomach with her cooking." Deacon paused and spat a glob of tobacco juice toward the fire, which was beginning to glow in the coming twilight.

Half-Moon Bear was not to be outbargained just yet. "White Dove will teach her the way of Ute women and of cooking."

Deacon grew a little bolder. "We have a string of fine horses. We will give you two for the woman. Except for our three and the woman's horse, you can have your pick."

"We would rather have the children of the white woman. Horses we can get from Cheyenne or Arapaho almost any night."

Richmond could not resist speaking. In spite of Deacon's request that he keep silent, he had to ask, "Why is a white woman so important to you that you would pass up good horses?"

"White Dove has graced my lodge for many years. She has given me children, and she is a good medicine woman. I have been pleased with her." Having spoken, Half-Moon Bear picked up his bow, which was bound in rattlesnake skin, and stood before the fire signifying that conversation was over for the day.

Back in their own camp, Richmond felt an urgency to stop the delays and take more positive action.

"Two Dogs, what's up with the Arapaho and with Shannon?"

"Arapaho become restless. Smell of so many ponies affects their heads, who knows what they will try. Shannon I have tracked into the camp of the Arapaho."

"Why would the Arapaho take in Shannon and that bunch?"

"Who knows, maybe Shannon promised to help them get the woman." It was Two Dogs's habit to speak the truth whether anyone wanted to hear it or not. He continued, "I think Arapaho will hold off for a day or two before they begin to raid. More than that, I do not know."

Deacon spoke to calm Richmond. "We will meet with Half-Moon Bear early tomorrow. Maybe we should try to move things along a little faster."

CHAPTER 16

OLIVIA felt the pressure building inside her. She tried to get information from the older woman. Nothing made much sense at first, as she tried to piece together comments she could obtain from White Dove. There were remarks about horse trading in conjunction with bits and pieces of White Dove's life with the Ute. Bit by bit, Olivia drew out of White Dove the woman's belief that Olivia's life would be a parallel of her own, and White Dove tried her best to convince Olivia that life with the Utes would not be bad. "They are good people, child. Your men try to bargain with horses. Maybe they will succeed, maybe they won't."

"You mean they're trying to trade horses for my life?"

"Not your life, but your freedom."

Olivia absently sat down on her pallet, hearing the squeals of children outside. She looked at White Dove and knew she could never let herself become the simpleton that she saw there. Anger filled her heart. She wanted to trust Richmond and Deacon to get her out of the mess she was in, but she sat still and looked back. For years, she had depended upon Von Chesterfield, and he had ultimately put her out in the streets of Denver. Then she had put herself under the protection of Forrest Bates. The outcome had been very nearly the same, in spite of his love for her. As the shadows grew long in the camp, and the tepee darkened, she knew she could not trust her life any further in someone else's hands.

White Dove had been long asleep on her pallet across the doorway when Olivia finally lay back upon her bed and stared at the small patch of stars visible through the smoke hole. She fell asleep with a plan, although it was a fragile one.

Half-Moon Bear was eager to meet with the white men. Their message to him told him their patience was growing thin. He decided it might be time to bring up the possibility of weapons thrown in with the horses. The years on and off the reservations had left many of his warriors with nothing more than bows and arrows.

The conversation had not much more than started underneath the elms when Richmond and Deacon became aware that Half-Moon Bear's eyes were riveted somewhere behind them. They turned to look in the direction of his stare. Richmond heard Deacon's soft exclamation, "Oh, Damn!" at about the same time he saw Olivia walking toward them. Her eyes were fixed on Half-Moon Bear as if she was oblivious of the other men about them. Her hair was braided Indian-style in two thick plumes that hung over her shoulders, framing her face. She moved gracefully in the soft leggings.

When she spoke, her voice was clear and determined. "Half-Moon Bear, I will not be traded like some brood mare. I am a human being, and you have humiliated me in front of my friends. I think you know the serious nature of that defiling act. I have heard that you threaten to keep me, as you have kept White Dove for many years. She speaks your name with reverence for the kind way in which she has been treated. Your so-called kind way has left White Dove a fragment of a human being. She performs her duties, but she has no joy in life. She barely has a life at all. That may be her way, but it is not mine. I paid for three of the horses that these men rode in with. The bills of sale are in my saddlebags. I can bargain for my own release. Leave my friends out of this."

Half-Moon Bear stole a look at Richmond and Deacon. He could not read much upon their faces except the same astonishment he felt. He could not reduce his stature to bargaining with a woman, but perhaps there was some other way. He spoke sternly to Richmond and Deacon. "There are three horses that belong to this woman?"

"They do." Deacon spoke truthfully, although he was afraid that by some twist of Indian logic Half-Moon Bear might just decide since the woman was his captive, so were her horses. He had not experienced anything like this before, and for a moment he wanted to curse Olivia for throwing his negotiations awry.

Half-Moon Bear knew vaguely what the woman meant when she referred to a bill of sale. His mind raced to see what good this could mean for him. "Which horses are yours?"

"The one I rode in on is not to be traded. The others are the black, the buckskin, and the brown one with a white stocking."

The Ute thought for a moment in silence. He motioned, and his companions disappeared, leaving him alone with the white men and the woman who still stood in front of him. The courage of the woman he had captured was something he could not fail to admire. He turned to the men who now stood watching him. "I know the black one is a good horse, good lungs, speed in him. I have watched him very close. So will the buckskin be good animal. Both as spirited as the woman you ride with. The brown I will give to White Dove as a gift from your woman." He thought for a moment. "I will leave you two extra horses to be sure you escape my enemies in the Arapaho camp. I will take two horses from you for the time you have wasted for me in dealing for horses that belonged to the woman." Half-Moon Bear felt happy enough with the gift of five horses that he decided to forgo any discussion of arms to be thrown in. He knew they would probably need all they had against his enemy, the Arapaho.

His good fortune was making him feel magnanimous. "To the east there is a pass, through steep mountain trails. It is very dangerous, but passable on good horses such as you have. In many places the trail is no more wide than the length of your arm. I do not think the Arapaho know of it. Right now, you should go. I think the Arapaho do not expect much to happen through the day. It is at night they watch us. Horse Standing will show you the way. The Mexican-Apache and his friends ride with the Arapaho, but they will not know the trail you will take. But you must watch for them on the other side." He gave Deacon a withering look, silencing him.

"We ride now," was the simple statement that Horse Standing made to them as they met near the horses with their few possessions. They left snaking through the trees, watching everything around them, not knowing if Half-Moon Bear had been wrong, and the Arapaho might be aware of their activities.

After a few hours, Horse Standing drew up. "Trail is up there." He motioned toward the scraggy side of a mountain with nothing but a few half-dead cedars still surviving on a steep slope of rock. In the deep silence of a mountain afternoon, a large rabbit scurried across the small meadow on their right. The Ute reached into a pouch, drew an arrow that he fit into his bow, and fired. The rabbit went down without a sound. "You must eat now. Once you start across, there is no stopping."

The Kiowa walked over and picked up the warm body and began skinning it while Deacon built a cooking fire at the center of a deep stand of fir.

Horse Standing mounted his horse and spoke to the four of them. "We will meet again, no doubt. Next time, as friends." He rode away.

"Well, we should eat fast and go." Deacon attended to the fire.

Richmond got out the frying pan and lard, preparing them for the rabbit, when the Kiowa walked up beside him. Without a word, the Kiowa pulled a pair of field glasses from underneath his shirt and a small packet of papers that he reached toward Richmond. Richmond recognized them as his identification papers.

"I'll be damned. You got all this from Shannon's camp." His smile was broad, but he could not understand the Kiowa's thinking for withholding it from him these last few days.

While the rabbit fried, he turned toward Olivia. "Are you sure you're all right?" He had not had much of a chance to talk to her since they left the Ute camp. She lowered her head for a moment, and Richmond placed his big, rough hand over hers. She looked up at him.

"Richmond, I guess I am a little scared." Her blue eyes were wide.

Before he knew it, Richmond's arms went around her, and he pulled her close to him.

"I guess I'm a little scared too, Olivia. I think we all are, except maybe for that Kiowa. But Half-Moon Bear would not have told us about this trail if he thought we could not make it."

"How can you be sure, Richmond? How can we trust him?"

"Sometimes, Olivia, you just know you can trust somebody. And sometimes you just don't have any choice anyway. I think we've got a lot of both situations here."

Olivia felt her composure returning. "I'm just glad it will be dark so I can't see how far the fall would be off that mountain."

"Nothing will happen, Olivia, at least not tonight on this mountain. We've got good horses. Just hold loose on Carly's reins and don't try to guide him. He's as interested as you are in making it across."

As they both rose, Deacon approached. "Well, as cold as it's gonna be tonight, we don't have to worry about runnin' across a rattler on the trail." He tossed a blanket to Olivia. "It don't smell none too good, ma'am, but around your shoulders, it'll feel just fine." He paused for a moment and looked toward the dark sky where the peak of the mountain lay hidden in black obscurity. Then he looked back over the

COLORADO RANSOM ■ 141

precipitous terrain they had behind them and realized it was mild countryside in comparison to what faced them in the dark hours to come. "If I was still a prayin' man, this would be the time for it." Then he shrugged and stalked off toward his horse.

An hour later, Olivia pulled the blanket more firmly around her shoulders. As they plodded along, the night was still and bitterly cold. She wondered sometimes if her shivering would be enough to distract Carly so that the two of them would go plunging over the edge of some precipice.

The trail had become terrifyingly narrow. There were places where she followed the example of Deacon, who rode just in front of her, and she bent over the neck of her horse to keep from being brushed off by overhanging rock. Sometimes a cloud would float across the moon, and the darkness would become thicker. At those times, she seemed enveloped in a cocoon of blackness, she and Carly moving along with only the sound of the well-placed hooves beneath her seeming real. She seemed suspended somewhere between the earth and the sky. Sometimes her eyes would pick up the glimmer of stars that seemed to hang on a horizon below her, winking and blinking in playful deception. Each time a stone went over the edge of the cliff, displaced by one of the hooves of their horses, Olivia would try to count the bounces until she could hear it no longer.

She leaned over Carly's big neck, holding the reins very loosely in her hands. Her face was only inches from the big horse. She breathed deeply of horse scent and tried to think of simple pleasures, picnics beside quiet streams, meals of roasted quail, the feel of a newborn colt beneath her hands. Olivia's eyes flew open when she heard Deacon's dun neigh in fright. Around the head of the horse and his rider was a black cloud, whirling and swishing and making shrill cries. The piercing sounds were combined with a whirring in the night air that unnerved even Carly, who suddenly planted his feet firmly and tossed his head, blowing heavily through his nostrils.

It took a few seconds before Olivia could make out that the surging cloud of whirling blackness was a colony of bats pouring out from a cave barely two feet above the level of Deacon's head. Deacon's horse began pawing the air, lifting his front feet perhaps three feet from the narrow trail, throwing Deacon into the perilous situation of tipping off the back of his mount and sliding hundreds of feet down toward a rocky death. As quickly as they had come, the bats darted away into the darkness, becoming small murky outlines in the moonlight, dispersing in all directions, their squeals dying out as they darted away over the canyon. Olivia breathed more easily, and she felt Carly's muscles relax as he began plodding on along the craggy trail.

When they reached the top of the pass, it was a soulless place marked only with rocks and boulders and mossy lichens that grew like velvet over the stones. They pulled their horses up into the lee of a large chunk of granite and dismounted. They soon had a small fire ablaze, and they huddled about it, spending the too few hours before dawn sleeping, taking turns on watch, and letting their horses regain their strength for the grueling trip down a steep incline when daybreak came.

"Wish we had mules," Richmond declared softly to no one in particular the next morning.

"How come?" came Deacon's response. "So we could have Apaches gathered around too for the feeding?"

Richmond looked at him quizzically.

"Don't you know yet that the Apache appetite favors a mule better than just about anything—a deer, buffalo, or even a nice roasted beef shank?" Deacon watched with a smile for the look of surprise that swept over Richmond's face.

They climbed into their saddles in the silvery morning light and swung their mounts down the perilous trail, feeling confident after a little rest and a light meal that an hour or two of dangerous riding should bring them to decent terrain again. It seemed a long ride to Olivia, who kept her eyes closed most of the time and let Carly pick his way gingerly down the mountainside. Gradually, she began to feel safer. She tried to occupy her mind in thinking about what direction they would take once down from the mountain, hoping that the Kiowa or Deacon knew of some route that would keep them from the Arapaho.

She was surprised to find herself thinking of confidence in Two Dogs. Looking back to the scene in Denver, she felt terribly ashamed for her words after the loyalty and skill that Two Dogs had exhibited. It made her feel better to think that perhaps Two Dogs did not feel offended, since he treated her pleasantly, just as if it had never happened. Both of them had been the object of insulting comments that morning.

Like Olivia, Richmond also frequently had the urge to close his eyes as the small group snaked around down the switchback trail. But he was captivated by the majestic scenery that unfolded beneath. He kept his eyes away from the steep pitch of the mountain at the edge of the switchbacks and let his eyes and soul drink in the dark mountains off to the east, where the sky was pinkening. Morning mists drifted in the valleys, wisps floating through the air in and out among the lower peaks, seeming to be chasing each other out of the valleys before the sun caught them and dispelled them all. High on a craggy, jutting rock slightly above him on the right, he glimpsed a black muzzle, massive curlicues of horn, and the stout body of a bighorn sheep. A large bird with an enormous wingspan floated between him and the coming light, and Richmond realized he was seeing his first eagle seeking a meal from among the hardy rodent population.

Watching the woman with the golden hair in front of him gave him a feeling of pride in her. She had been through more than he could even imagine yet, since they had had little time to talk, but she endured. The slim taper of her body melting into the saddle made him realize the fragility that he would have expected to find within this woman, but that had somehow been replaced by a strength people called grit. It summed up her spirit and endurance, grit.

Olivia began opening one eye from time to time in order to see if any end to the treacherous pathway was in sight. She let out her breath with a low sigh when, on the outer edge of a switchback, she caught sight of meadowland perhaps a hundred yards away beneath them. Her legs trembled slightly when she could finally dismount and walk about on the soft carpet of grass.

While they stretched their legs, Richmond used the time to question Deacon. "Well, what do you think? Shannon and them Arapaho goin' to come after us or what?"

"Likely. I've been thinkin' about it. I figure Shannon and Poncho know we're goin' to your place. Nothin' left for us in Denver right now. Well, we could ride all the way to your place and not see hide nor hair of them, then find them sittin' on the doorstep when we ride up. Or we could find them around the bend in the trail that we next come to. I reckon, though, that they lost a half day or more on us by followin' around the base of this mountain.

"If it was just the Indians, I'd say they wouldn't think our few ponies are worth the chase. And Indians by nature are not partial to gold like the white man. But with Shannon and the Mex to lather them up, I'm not sure what to expect."

"Deacon, do you think we could shake them up a little, providing they end up on our trail, by slipping around a little like we might be going to Denver and then make a run for it to the cabin?"

"Well, can't see no reason not to try it. I don't have a better plan myself." He looked toward Two Dogs, but there was no expression on the Kiowa's face to indicate disagreement.

They snaked up toward Denver for a while, making a wide path for anyone to follow easily, covering some ten to fifteen miles that day. They came across a streambed that would serve their purposes with three to four inches of water running. Then they cut back in the direction of The Lucky Lady. By nightfall, they had found a low valley where the horses could be staked in good grass.

The Kiowa came slipping back into camp just after daybreak the next morning with news they had been dreading to hear.

"Riders coming, two white men maybe half-mile away."

"Two Dogs, are they followin' our trail or just ridin'?" Deacon asked.

"Ridin' trail."

In no time, Richmond and Deacon had positioned themselves in a casual-looking manner around the camp, but in strategic locations so if firing began, cover was only a matter of rolling over onto their sides and disappearing into thick brush. The Kiowa disappeared into the trees, and Olivia knelt as if she were tending fire, ready to hide herself before the riders got into rifle range. She began to feed pine slivers into the tiny blaze for kindling.

Two horsemen soon rode into view and stopped just outside the stand of trees across the meadow. They sat still long enough to know they would not arouse a swift bullet out of a surprised camp, then they walked their horses a little closer.

Olivia watched them approach. The horses were brown, stout-looking animals. The left horse had a white stocking on the left foreleg and the right hind. A soft white patch was on his shoulder. A voice rang across the valley: "Hello, the camp!"

Olivia raced toward the animals and the men, yelling back over her shoulder, "Richmond, the Bishops!"

When the handshaking and introductions were over, Dave explained their presence. "We've been cuttin' your trail, here and there, since yesterday sometime."

"Then Ike must have found you when we sent him back."

To Richmond it seemed it must have been a hundred years since they last saw Ike taking off toward Wells Springs.

"Well, not exactly. One of our riders found Ike. He fetched him back to the ranch, and we buried him proper. We started to look around for you and Miss Olivia, and we've just been workin' the ranch when Ma had to have us and lopin' these hills hopin' to find some sign of you. We found Miss Olivia's mare and the mules. We taken them back to the ranch. We knowed if we looked long enough, we'd likely find you."

Over a hearty breakfast of salt pork, gravy, and biscuits baked in a heavy iron skillet that Dave swore he never traveled without, the Bishops were filled in with all the events that had occurred since Ike's death. The young men shoveled food into their mouths while hearing about the attack by Shannon and the encounter with the Indians.

Bob put his cup down on a flat rock. "Well, let's go get 'em. We had plenty of trouble with Arapaho down on the ranch, and chances are they're ridin' some of our Slinging Six horses right now."

Dave backed' him up. "Amen, brother, let's go get 'em. We're a match for them Arapaho any day, all of us. Why, Miss Olivia can hold her own against them Arapaho, I'd bet." He tipped his battered hat toward her.

Her smile back at Dave made Richmond's breakfast turn into a hard knot in his stomach, but he never let it show.

"Wait, boys, let's not be too quick about this." He was alarmed at their haste to be in pursuit of a band of Indians. "I can't go chasin' off after a bunch of Indians that may not even be after us anymore. I've got to think about getting Olivia back home and laying legal claim to my uncle's property. We've got to establish our right to that mine."

"After we get done with them Indians, Miss Olivia might have no need for Forrest Bates's property." Dave spoke while staring at Olivia with a frank hunger in his eyes.

Olivia blushed and looked away, while Richmond gazed at Dave with hostility. A slow red had begun at the base of

Richmond's neck and had spread upward to encompass his face and ears. "What's that mean, Bishop?"

Dave caught the tension in Richmond's voice and realized he had gone too far. He had never met Richmond Bates before, so had never considered that he might be interested in his uncle's girl. He found it was his turn to blush. "Nothin', Bates. I didn't mean nothin'."

Deacon broke into the exchange at this time with a cool head. "Okay, what's it to be? You guys goin' after the Indians, or we goin' for the mine?" He knew what he was going to do.

Bob Bishop had been watching with amusement the brief flare-up between Richmond and his brother. Now his thoughts got more serious. "That Poncho, I've heard about him. That man won't give up on you. Shannon might, the Arapaho might, but when Poncho gets a grudge, I hear he follers it through. Seems he's had a burr under his saddle since the trouble, the massacre some say, of the Arivaipa Apache down toward Ole Pueblo. It happened in the spring of 'seventy-one, and he's been out for whites ever since. I don't know if he lost family or what's eatin' him, but you're not likely to shake him for good if you've got him mad. You'll end up killin' or bein' killed, Bates."

It was a sobering thought for all of them. Richmond said, "Well, let's get back to The Lucky Lady. I'll meet him on my own ground and not out spookin' around in country he knows a hell of a lot better than I do."

PART V

Standing Ground

CHAPTER 17

ALTHOUGH they made good time in getting back to The Lucky Lady, Richmond had time to think about Dave's inference regarding Olivia. Dave had acted as if he was trying to set claim on her, Richmond thought. He knew he would be happiest to take Olivia back to Arkansas and have a good life on his farm. He would never be a man of wealth there, but at least he and Olivia would be free of the likes of Shannon and Poncho. He pondered why it had taken him so many years and so many miles to find a woman that interested him.

In spite of his shyness, he knew he had to look for a chance to be alone with Olivia. He finally found it. The day was a bright one; halfway through the morning, the party had slowed their horses to a walk to give them a rest. Olivia and Richmond were riding at the back of the procession.

"Richmond, I know you are planning to go back and rebury Forrest, just like you were before."

"No, Olivia, I don't think I'm planning in that direction anymore. It doesn't seem to matter now. I had figured that maybe Uncle Forrest was murdered; I reckon I know now. And I know I should have killed Shannon and Poncho and Juan when I had the chance. But I guess Forrest will rest easy where he is." He spoke calmly. "What matters now is us. Olivia, can we be married?" His voice had taken on a hoarse sound, and his face was as pink as a Colorado sunrise. He knew this was the wrong way to go about a proposal of marriage, but he knew he had to seize his opportunity. "I know I can take care of you with or without Forrest's property. I'd be mighty proud to take you home with me. My farm is good land. We would have a decent life." He knew his rambling sounded as if his mind was slightly off center, and maybe it really was. He pulled his horse up, realizing the seriousness of this moment and waiting for her to answer.

Olivia took a few moments to think. She had not been taken totally by surprise by this proposal, but she had not expected it so soon. Since the first night in the cabin, she had known Richmond was attracted to her as she had been to him. They had depended upon each other on the trail and had been through a lifetime's worth of danger and turmoil. But she felt it was too early after too many things had been happening in her life to be able to make a commitment for the rest of her life.

"Richmond, I am touched by your proposal, and I care very deeply for you." She spoke carefully, weighing each word. "Any woman should be proud to be your wife, but I cannot say yes just now. I can't say yes and I can't say no." She searched her mind for the words to define her reluctance to commit herself at this time. She still felt a bond with Forrest, although she had never loved him as a wife should love a husband. The tumult in her life since Forrest's death had left no time for much more than survival. She turned to Richmond with a soft smile. "Thank you, Richmond. Can we talk about this again after we get home?"

Richmond nodded and felt rather foolish, hoping he had not made her too uncomfortable. He searched for words that would not come. They urged their horses forward to catch up with the others.

Olivia had spent the hours in the Indian camp and on the trail assessing many things. One of the major things she had come to grips with was her treatment of Two Dogs in Denver, but now she felt a sense of peace over that situation. The Ute had been somewhat harsh with her, but not unkind. They were completely different from her memories of the raging savages who had killed her family. She felt some sense of satisfaction in dealing with her release from Half-Moon Bear's camp as she had done. She realized that Deacon

Romine could have probably obtained her release for fewer horses, and she knew he probably resented her intrusion a good deal; but she didn't care. Her self-respect was worth more than a few animals to her, if not to Deacon. He had lost nothing that was his in the trade; she had stood to lose something very precious to her if she had sat idly by hoping for her benefactors to have provided a safe negotiation for her freedom.

She found herself with something she had never had before—a chance to plan the rest of her life, instead of being grateful for what someone provided to her. The opportunity for a choice in life was an overwhelming force for her to deal with now. The bank account in Denver was a large factor that gave her a sense of independence, although the money might be a paltry sum to many. Richmond's proposal, while not a surprise, created more questions she had to face soon, and for the rest of the journey to The Lucky Lady, she tried to keep to herself to ponder alone.

Richmond was not the only one of the party having amorous thoughts. After they had arrived at The Lucky Lady and had spent a couple of days with nothing disturbing the quiet except a bear that ambled up one night and set the horses to screaming and kicking, they awoke one morning to find Two Dogs gone. His being away was not unusual, but the fact that he didn't return within a few days was beginning to set the three others to worrying. By the second morning, Richmond and Deacon decided to take turns trying to track the Kiowa. Neither had much luck.

"Oh, well," Deacon finally said, "maybe he just got restless and took off, though I've always figgered him for a stayer. You just never know about Indians." He and Richmond continued their work in the mine.

The morning of the fifth or sixth day of Two Dogs's absence brought a change. Deacon was washing his face in a basin of water on the porch, when something near the trees caught his eye. He dropped the towel he had been holding and got his gun hand into position while he stared at two figures seated on horses. "My God Almighty! Richmond, get out here!"

Richmond came outside, reaching for his gun. "What's wrong?"

"Richmond, I don't know if anything is wrong. But that there's Two Dogs, and if my eyes haven't left me, that companion of his is a woman I remember from Half-Moon Bear's camp."

"Oh, hell! I think you're right!"

There was a big smile on Two Dogs's usually somber face as he enjoyed the surprised looks on the two men's faces. The two Indians rode up close.

"This is Little Feather of the Ute," Two Dogs announced.

"My God, Two Dogs, where'd you get her?" Deacon looked admiringly at the young Indian woman who sat serenely astride her horse while the two white men gaped and stared at her.

"I got her from Ute camp." Two Dogs baited Richmond and Deacon, knowing they would appreciate his woman's beauty as they tried to drag out the explanation of her presence.

"Well, Two Dogs, I hope the Ute are not camped by close enough for you to just ride in and steal her away." Richmond tore his eyes from the girl and looked toward the forest.

Little Feather could see that Two Dogs was deliberately tormenting his friends, but she felt it had gone far enough. She gave a sparkling laugh and said, "We had plan to meet. He did not kidnap me. I left Ute willingly to be with him." She turned her eyes toward Two Dogs with a gaze that Richmond thought was uncommonly lustful for a young woman.

The atmosphere around The Lucky Lady and the cabin changed with the lovers in their midst. Olivia watched Two

Dogs and Little Feather engaging in lovers' play and teasing, and she watched Richmond watching them also. On one hand, she wanted to accept his proposal, but she found herself keeping away from him, avoiding possible situations that could lead to intimate discussions. She could not explain her feelings to herself yet, much less to another person.

Tensions also were high among Richmond, Deacon, and Olivia—they lived daily in expectation of a visit from Roy Shannon, Poncho, and Juan. Richmond steadfastly held out that he would wait there until the thieves came to him. Deacon reluctantly agreed; besides, it felt good to him to be back in a mine once again, earning what he felt was an honest living. Two Dogs was practically useless with a pick or shovel, so he was left to scout and guard and hunt when he was not sneaking away to romance Little Feather. Richmond grew more homesick every day wondering how things were faring at home. He yearned for something that was green and grew from day to day, instead of the lifeless lumps of rock he was dealing with.

The three of them were joyful when they learned of a party to be held at The Golden Dog. Ross Miles's son had recently married, and he was bringing his bride west to meet his father. The people of Wells Springs did not have many occasions to celebrate, and this was the best excuse they had come upon in some time. Two Dogs and Little Feather looked forward to a day alone, and Two Dogs figured he could get in a little hunting before the revelers returned home.

In the small alcove that served as a café, Sarah Lamont and a few women with starched bonnets clustered around a couple of tables with slightly yellowed lace cloths. On one there was a punch bowl holding some languid-looking pink beverage that Mrs. Bishop had prepared, and on the other was a large chocolate cake flanked with an assortment of cupcakes and doughnuts. The frosting on the cake held up fairly well in the afternoon warmth, drooping only a little before the delicacy began to disappear as the party got under way. Ross Miles's son Milam and his rosy-cheeked bride, Mary Lee, stood beside the serving table dutifully shaking hands and smiling, pleased with their reception in Wells Springs.

The action was a little more lively in Earl's half of the establishment. The bartender was a busy man as the men bellied up to the bar and ordered drinks, to be paid for by Ross Miles. Richmond was among them, recognizing but few of the men, but enjoying the talk and laughter. He had had his fill of lonely nights up at the cabin wondering when Shannon would strike and thinking about the lovely lady in the bed in the same room where his pallet lay on the floor. He tilted his beer mug again and again.

Deacon likewise enjoyed the rare party. Although he liked the work in the mine, he had grown restless waiting for the trip into Denver to file the will. He agreed it was not a move they should make just yet. Like Richmond, he did not want to risk a meeting with Shannon and his men out on the trail. It was better to bide their time near home and wait for the meeting. When anyone except Two Dogs rode out from the cabin or the mine, by Deacon's orders, it was never alone, and it was always with full arms. Many times lately, Two Dogs had sighted prints of a big horse, tracks that appeared often and in many places. Occasionally, large footprints of a heavy man were around the prints of the horse, and sometimes the bushes would carry a few long, dark-brown hairs from a horse's tail. Sometimes it was evident that other horses, both shod and unshod, rode with the big horse. It had been enough to keep them all close to home. On more than one occasion, Deacon had been inclined to ride out seeking their adversaries, but he knew that was a rash thought. It would be better to let them come to him and Richmond.

With full arms, they rode into town for the celebration, and headed out early before the festivities were over.

Olivia was astride Ribbon in a riding skirt and cantering up the trail toward the cabin when the bullet struck Ribbon

COLORADO RANSOM ■ 157

just behind the right ear through the top of the neck. The little mare let out a frightened shriek, and without any urging from Olivia pursued the trail ahead with hooves flying. Olivia had been riding beside Richmond, so she figured Ribbon had taken a bullet intended for him. Rubbing Ribbon's neck, Olivia could feel sticky blood. She bent low in the saddle and talked comfortingly to the mare, terrified that this could be a mortal injury to her little horse. The trees whisked by on either side, and she hoped she had left behind those who shot at her. Calming her heart a bit by listening to the reassuring pound of Ribbon's hooves, she heard shots behind her.

She soon saw the cabin, looking serene in the glow of the fading afternoon sunlight. She hoped Two Dogs was there. Slowing Ribbon to a trot and stopping the horse just off the porch, she jumped down as Little Feather opened the door. With a soft tug, she coaxed the puzzled little mare up onto the porch. Ribbon lowered her head as she began to understand what her mistress was commanding and passed through the door into the cabin.

Olivia looked around for Two Dogs. Little Feather understood what she was seeking. "He is hunting. I thought he would be back by now." Fear for Two Dogs showed in here eyes. She spoke softly while she stared at the small droplets of blood falling from Ribbon's mane onto the rough floor. "I heard shots. What has happened?" Quickly, her fingers started feeling the mare's neck, who stood calmly as if she were in her own stall.

While Olivia dropped a heavy two-by-four into the stout braces on the wall, making the door a strong barrier, she quickly explained the gunshots from the forest to Little Feather. Looking about, she could see that the young Indian woman had secured the window shutters. She looked at the horse.

Little Feather's words were comforting. "Ribbon will be well. Shot hit only a bleeder at the top of her neck."

Olivia began to feel guilty that she was not out there taking part in the fight, although Ribbon had not asked her permission before she started to run. Olivia knew she probably could have stopped her, unlike the headstrong Carly. She fought against the urge to go back to try to help. She hoped Two Dogs was close enough to hear the firing.

"It has to be Shannon and Poncho and some ragged group of thieves and killers."

Quietly, Olivia pulled the saddle off Ribbon. Little Feather mixed some kind of concoction from some small deerskin pouches with a little water and then applied it to Ribbon's wound.

The whine of a bullet striking the side of the cabin sang out, and the two jumped at the same time as they heard the sound of a horse beating up the trail. Richmond and Deacon plunged from their horses as they swooped by the porch. Each man slapped the rump of his horse to send them galloping away. Little Feather opened the door as soon as the men's boots hit the planks, and Olivia stood by with her rifle while the men flung themselves into the house.

"Deacon, my God! You're hurt!" The front of his shirt was bloodied, and he looked weak. Olivia led him to a chair and began pulling at his shirt buttons.

"Olivia, this is nothin'." His voice ended in a sigh as he slid off the chair and onto the floor.

Little Feather looked with questioning eyes at Richmond. "He's out there, Little Feather. He must've heard the shots. Last I saw of Two Dogs, he was slipping off through the trees on that horse of his that moves like midnight silence." He tried to sound reassuring for her. "He'll be okay. I know he will. Now, please, look after Deacon." After a quick glance at Ribbon standing toward the back of the room, Richmond said not a word, as if he was used to horses sharing the room with them.

The women did not bother to move Deacon toward the bed but left him on the floor near the kitchen table where he had fallen while they stripped off his shirt by the light of a kerosene lantern. The late-afternoon darkness made the place look gloomy. A hole pierced Deacon's chest just underneath his left shoulder. They knew from the blood pooling on the floor underneath him that the shot had gone through.

Richmond walked from side to side listening for any sounds outside. The quiet was onimous. He tried to figure out what the men would be doing. As near as he could count, there had been six of them, and they had not looked as though they were in the mood to take hostages or dicker over possession of a will. He turned back to the women. "All right, just pour a good slug from Two Dogs's whiskey bottle into that hole, and be ready to stand back in case he is the least bit conscious. Hope to hell he's still out of it. It'll hurt a little."

Deacon moaned a little when the whiskey hit the raw wound, but he remained still. Again, Little Feather mixed some powders and packed them into the bullet hole, just as she had done with the horse. This would stop the bleeding. When Little Feather finished dressing the wound and binding the shoulder with strips from a soft blanket, she looked toward Olivia with a reassuring nod. Little Feather knew that in spite of the man's gruffness, Olivia had developed a strong respect and affection for him.

Little Feather stopped quickly and stood totally still, cocking her head to one side. "The sound of the mountain grouse. It's Two Dogs." She moved over to the door and opened it just a crack and let out a small cry that sounded like a caught rabbit. Two Dogs drifted around the side of the cabin and into the door, much as a cloud moves like a shadow across the face of the moon.

Two Dogs spoke quickly. "They leave two guards. One at west corner of corral. Other is across from him in lodgepole pines. We are in crossfire. Shannon and others go to mine."

There was a good-sized haul of ore that Richmond and Deacon had pulled out of The Lucky Lady the past few weeks and had left within the mouth of the mine. No one yet knew the value of the ore, because Forrest's records had not been too plain on the value he estimated within the vein.

Richmond stood up. "I don't care if there ain't but ten dollars' worth of gold in that pile of ore, Roy Shannon's not going to get it!" He strode to the back of the cabin and pulled some loose boards from the floor. Forrest had dug a good-sized hole and lined it thickly with hay to keep his dynamite free from moisture. "Grab a few sticks, Two Dogs."

"Richmond, you can't blow up the mine!" Olivia exclaimed.

"Olivia, would you mind if I blow up the corner post on the corral? Or if I blow up that little stand of lodgepole out there?" Tension made his voice ring with sarcasm.

Now Olivia understood his plan. "No, I don't think I would mind that. Then I'll need to be out there for cover."

"You're right. I hate to ask it, but we can expect them to come scootin' down that mountain quicker than greased lightning when they hear this dynamite go off. With the three of us, maybe we can catch them before they get off much more than a shot or two. Let's wait for good dark." Richmond spoke truthfully when he said he hated to ask Olivia for this kind of help, but he knew that he probably couldn't keep Olivia out of the fracas even if he didn't desperately need her firing power. He could only trust her to be careful. He knew he was fighting for more than a few dollars' worth of ore. He could no longer stand the worry every time Olivia got out of sight of the house. He had to get the threat of Roy Shannon out of their lives.

Soon full darkness began to close in. Little Feather turned the lantern down and moved it to the back of the room. The fire had burned down to dark coals. Two Dogs and Richmond could open the door just a sliver and slip out without the light pouring through the doorway.

Olivia and Little Feather sat quietly and waited for the sounds of explosions. They came only seconds apart, close enough that the dishes rattled on the shelves. Ribbon tossed her head but remained quiet. Olivia slid out the door with her rifle, leaving Little Feather with two loaded guns beside her. Olivia ran swiftly through the chill of the night.

She reached the chosen spot barely seconds before she heard the horses pounding down the steep trail from the mine. Olivia peered around the thick trunk of a huge pine, while Richmond waited atop a big clump of granite that rose out of the earth near the trail. The large, rocky formation had two small peaks atop it that made a handy crevice in which his rifle could be propped. Two Dogs had gone a little farther up the trail to make sure none of them escaped from the way they would come.

Shannon and Poncho were in the lead as the four bandits rushed down the trail. Olivia could make out the pock-marked face in the dim light and could see the misplaced teeth that always made his face look as if it wore an evil grin. They held their fire until all four were in sight. Poncho was the first to go, his ugly face smattered by a piercing blast from Richmond's rifle.

Olivia started firing at the same time as the bark from Two Dogs's Henry sounded through the night. At the sound of the firing, Shannon and the two other men dived from their horses, returning shots almost before they hit the ground. After the first volleys had been fired, Olivia held her fire as she had been told to do. From the darkness, she watched as well as she could the progress of the gunfight, ready to shoot if it looked as if Two Dogs or Richmond was threatened. One of the men was dispatched before he could reach the cover of the trees. Olivia wasn't sure, but it looked like Juan. Before long, Olivia could tell that only one gun was being fired at Richmond. She wondered if that was the only one alive. From the direction of the last two volleys, it seemed that Shannon must be the last one to continue shooting.

Richmond stopped firing, and his voice rang out. "Is that you, Shannon?" There was no response. "You can surrender, Shannon. Throw that gun down and come on out." The only answer was a bullet sent whining off the rock near Richmond's head. Richmond wanted to keep him distracted with talk. "Shannon, come out and take your chances in a court of law. At least that way you'd have a chance. This way, you know we'll get you."

A long period of silence followed, then a rustle of bushes in the direction from which Shannon had been firing. Two Dogs's voice came through the darkness: "I guess we got 'em all." He cleared the bushes, dragging Roy Shannon's body with him and wiping his bloody knife on the dead man's shirt. He dumped Shannon's corpse in the middle of the trail and then dragged the other bodies together. When he came to Poncho, he lay facedown. Two Dogs reached out and flipped him over with his right foot. The body flopped over like a sack of flour with arms. The corpses looked gray and still in the moonlight. "Guess we blew those other two to smithereens."

Olivia turned away in case Two Dogs decided to take other adornments for the thong around his neck. And she did not want Richmond and Two Dogs to see the tears gathering in her eyes, tears of relief. Leaving the men to make whatever plans they wanted to for the disposal of the bodies, she walked very slowly back to the cabin.

Inside, she could see that Deacon still slept. She gathered Ribbon's reins and led her out the door and toward the barn, feeling slightly foolish now for having taken the mare into the house. She lit a lantern and spread some grain in the bin. As the mare ate, Olivia put her head down on her soft mane and wept. Olivia drew comfort from the sturdy warmth of the animal as her tears wet the side of Ribbon's neck. When her tears had subsided and the horse was comfortable for the night, Olivia blew out the lantern.

She stood alone outside the barn for a few minutes, staring up the dark hillside in the direction of The Lucky Lady. She knew now she didn't have to avoid being alone with Richmond as she had been doing lately.

CHAPTER 18

AS soon as Deacon Romine was back on his feet, Richmond set off alone to Denver. He took with him Forrest's will and a letter from Ross Miles to serve as proof of his uncle's death. This trip was much more successful than his previous encounter with banking officials had been. With no problem, he was able to get the bank account and Forrest's mine registered as he wanted them, in the names of Richmond Bates and Olivia Palmer. He had not told Olivia that he intended to make the properties in both their names, because he knew she would object. Richmond knew he could not have it any other way. The property was rightfully theirs, not his. He knew this time he was going to be as stubborn as she about something that mattered very much to him. Olivia should know that her future was secure, with or without a husband.

On the long ride back to The Lucky Lady, he pondered what he should do next and still had not come up with a satisfying answer by the time he arrived.

He had to make some decision soon, for there were preparations to be made at home before winter.

If things had been different, he would have put away enough dried game to have seen them through the worst winter. The barn would have been filled with hay from the Slinging Six, and firewood would have been stacked high.

Deacon and Two Dogs had said nothing about leaving. They seemed content to leave the trail riding to someone else for now. Two Dogs spent much of his day hunting, bringing in game that Little Feather dried and preserved. Little Feather frequently took time to scan the forest for edible plants and those with medicinal qualities. Olivia trailed along, eager to learn anything she could.

Deacon watched and wondered. From his tiny room, a boarded-up stall in the barn, he watched Two Dogs and Little Feather retire each night to their bed of boughs in the tack room at the eastern end of the barn. At first, he had expected to wake up any morning and find that they had packed their horses and were leaving for the Indian life again, perhaps with her people, perhaps his. As the days wore on and they stayed, Deacon began to feel that they planned to stay through the winter. He watched Richmond go about his work each day as if he did not realize that winter would be coming soon.

Deacon finally began wondering about himself. Here he was, acting like a miner. He, who had ridden the hills with some sort of aimless mission of revenge for years, found himself waking before daylight each day to cleave and hack in the darkness of the mine all day and return to his tiny room each night after supper too tired to even think about his own future. But somehow he found himself liking it. He knew where his bed would be each night, that the women would see that it was clean and that he had a good supper in the warmth and cheer of the cabin. He wondered about asking Richmond if he could winter here.

It was finally Richmond who brought it up. The day had been warm when he came out of the mine at midmorning to stretch his back and shoulder muscles, but a chilly breeze was stirring the tops of the pines. With a sudden seriousness, he knew he had to face a decision soon. He returned to the mine with his pick and worked feverishly on the walls of the tunnel, digging and scraping, stopping only when Deacon asked him for a hand with the timbers.

Deacon could see that his behavior was unusual, for Richmond usually worked methodically, not at a frenzied pace. He said nothing, however, and worked quietly with the shoring while Richmond's pick flew randomly over the rocks.

Noontime brought them outdoors again, where the sun had disappeared and the wind blew colder, now rustling along through the trunks of the trees while clouds drifted low.

"Dammit, Deacon, I don't know anything about mining. Sometimes I wonder what I'm doin' here!"

Deacon had wondered the same thing many times, but he didn't think it was the time to tell Richmond of his musings. "Well, Richmond, by comin' out here, you got yourself a fine little woman and a gold mine. You could've done worse, you know. You could've got a arrow in your back and your scalp lifted. You ain't done too bad."

Richmond squatted over his heels, not appreciating Deacon's wit just now. "I'm not sure I've got the fine little woman, as you call her. She hasn't agreed to marry me yet."

"Maybe you ought to ask her again. She knows winter's comin'. A woman like Olivia, never havin' a home of her own, she might take to sittin' on the front porch down in Arkansas, watchin' the cotton grow and slappin' them southern muskeeters that folks have told me about."

The thought made Richmond grin. He could never see Olivia being happy to sit idly anywhere. He picked up a handful of pebbles and tossed them one at a time toward a rusty tin cup that lay near a tangle of brush a few yards off, listening distantly to the pings as he considered Deacon's comment.

"But what about the mine? No sane man would walk away from a gold mine that might turn out to be a durn good payin' one."

"Well, I've been watchin' Two Dogs and Little Feather. They seem right content here. Me, too, for that matter," he confessed. "I reckon we could work out some arrangement to look out for your property for a while, least 'til spring. By then you might be back or we might be a couple of seasoned miners and ready to light somewhere for a long spell."

Richmond knew he was right.

That night after supper, he asked Olivia if she would like to go for a walk.

She looked surprised, but grabbed a jacket quickly.

The night was chilly but filled with stars as they strolled under the trees.

"I thought we needed to talk, Olivia."

"Yes, Richmond, we do." She moved closer to him, and he felt her shiver.

He put his arm around her shoulder. He found her walking toward the barn. "Let's slip inside, Richmond. It'll be warmer in there."

The next thing he knew, they were lying on a pile of hay. His arms were about her, rubbing her back, caressing her hair.

She whispered, "We can talk tomorrow."

Then they became a tangle of arms, legs, and bodies burrowing into the straw, whispering their love to each other.

When Richmond arose the next morning, Olivia met him in the kitchen with a mellow smile. "Good morning, Richmond. You are right. We do need to talk. Do you think you could take some time away from the mine today? I think it might be warm enough for a little picnic."

He smiled and nodded, remembering the night before. "I'll tell Deacon."

While she prepared breakfast, Olivia also fried the breasts of three quail Two Dogs had brought in the previous day and packed them in a small basket along with some fry bread that Little Feather had made. She started to put in some onions, but thought better of it and replaced them with a chunk of cheese.

It was cool and brisk when they rode out. Olivia shivered slightly and pulled her jacket more closely around her. She glanced up at The Lucky Lady and felt glad to be alive.

Richmond rode quietly with his own thoughts. Until last night in the hay, he had never actually told Olivia that he loved her. That sat hard with him, and he wondered how much her decision regarding their future had been tainted by his omission. He started to blurt out now his declarations of love, but the idea made him uncomfortable, and he figured it would do the same to her. He kept quiet and rode along wondering what else he should say. He noticed that Olivia had taken special care of her appearance this morning. She wore the riding skirt that he had first seen her in when she rode up to the cabin the first morning of their meeting. Her hair was brushed to a satin sheen, and it fell loosely down her back, making her look fresh and innocent.

When they found the place she sought for the picnic, they spread the blanket in a sunlit clearing where clumps of sage grew from between the rocks and the coarse soil was warm to the hand. He drew Olivia to him and kissed her slowly.

She returned his kiss, but not with the passion of the night before. She pulled gently from his arms.

"Richmond, I have decided that I cannot accept your proposal of marriage right now. There are many reasons for this, which I will try to explain to you."

They sat down on the blanket and Richmond halfway reclined, propped up on an elbow so that he could see her face. She reached out now and rubbed her index finger along the side of his face. "I admit that I had strong second thoughts about my decision after last night. It was the first time you have told me you loved me, but I guess I have known that for a long time. And I think I have returned that love. I think, Richmond, but I can't be positive right now. You see, since I was just a girl, I've had a man in my life to take care of me, first Von Chesterfield and then, briefly, Forrest. After each of them I was left alone again and had to try to learn to take care of myself all over. When I was in that Indian camp, my life was dependent on somebody else's whim. I began to know then that I had to take care of myself.

"I've never been in love with a man before. My relationship with Von Chesterfield was a matter of survival for a young girl. And in a way, so was my relationship with Forrest, although he was a wonderful person, and I cared for him very much. I know I am rambling, but I don't want you to be hurt, so you must understand." She stopped before her voice became choked with tears.

This was not what Richmond had wanted to hear, but he could read the sincerity in her face as she struggled slowly to find exactly the right words to convey her meaning.

He started to speak, but she held up her hand toward him.

"Let me go on just a bit more, please. Will you accept my answer that I cannot marry you now? Perhaps in the spring or next year . . . perhaps never."

"What else can I do, Olivia? I'm thirty-two years old and have never asked a woman to marry me; I've never considered it. I'm not likely to change my mind once it's made up. What do you want to do?"

"I want to stay here for now." Her voice sounded lighter. "It seems to me that Deacon and Two Dogs want to do the same for a while; maybe they're getting tired of roaming the hills. Deacon could work the mine for you as much as the winter will allow. Even if the three of them leave, I'll be all right here alone. Can you believe how scared I was of traveling with an Indian a few months ago, and now I want to share a life with Two Dogs and Little Feather?"

She smiled, and Richmond realized how much she had brightened up with the talk about staying on at The Lucky Lady. Richmond knew he had made the right decision about the division of property. It was apparent she was very fond of this place and she felt it was going to be her home for now.

However, it took a fiery discussion to convince Olivia that it was the right and proper thing he had done when he told her she was the half-owner of The Lucky Lady and all of Forrest's property. From her reaction, it would have seemed that someone had taken valuable property from her instead of otherwise. It took Richmond several minutes of listening to her rage for him to begin to comprehend that she saw herself again as a kept woman.

They were both standing by now, and he took her gently by the shoulders. "Olivia, have the courtesy to allow me to explain why I feel you are rightfully entitled to half of Forrest's things."

At his appeal to her manners, she quietened.

"You made my uncle very happy. He wanted to marry you. If you had accepted, the whole place would have been yours, just the way he would have wanted it. If it had not been for your help, I likely wouldn't be alive to own this property or ever go back to my farm. Olivia, you probably deserve the whole damn thing instead of half." His voice became gentler, and she allowed him to pull her into his arms. "But you see, this way, you're my partner, and I don't think you would ever run out on a partner."

He heard a little sob catch in her throat, and he had to swallow hard, too, as he stood holding her.

Then he tried to make her mood lighter. "Olivia, I hope by spring you'll tell me I can come and get you. I have thought so much about how proud I would be to show you off at home. I saw an outfit in Denver that would make heads turn in Washington, Arkansas. I want to take you home with you wearing a dress of cranberry-colored velvet, with a full skirt, the top cut low, down to about here." His fingers traced a line across the middle of her breasts, making her nipples stand out behind her shirt. "Maybe you'll need a little hat of some kind to go with the dress." He smiled with mischief. "I'll bet I can even buy you a horse with spots that will match your new dress!"

She smiled at him with little tears gathering in the corners of her eyes. "Richmond, you know there is no such thing as a horse with cranberry spots."

"We'll see, Olivia." If she would marry him, he knew he would realize his dreams—even if that meant finding a horse with cranberry spots.

If you have enjoyed this book and would like to receive details on other Walker Western titles, please write to:

Western Editor
Walker and Company
720 Fifth Avenue
New York, NY 10019